A *Confusion* of Murders

Marina Johnson

DEDICATION

For PG and CJ, who made it possible.

Chapter One

If anyone had told me three years ago that I'd be working as a finance clerk in a scruffy newspaper office I would have laughed – although probably not as much as my old colleagues at the shiny corporate company where I used to work. The Frogham Herald started off as just one more in a long line of temporary jobs but there was something about the place that I liked and a year later, I'm still here.

There are only five of us at the Herald plus two printers who run the press. The Herald looks quite impressive from the front; all grand stone columns and heavy oak doors, but it's all for show, the doors don't even open. The real entrance is round the back through the scruffy car park, past the bins and in through a scuffed and chipped doorway and up the stairs.

Full to bursting with dusty grey filing cabinets, hundreds of box files and probably a million spiders, the inside is definitely *not* for show. My desk is the tidiest in the office and the only one that has a window, which now, clean of murk, has a view of the shopping precinct.

So, here I am, ten to nine, seated and ready for work.

Rupert, our not so roving reporter, his considerable bulk wedged into his swivel chair, is attempting to put his feet up on the desk while balancing a bacon sandwich and a mug of coffee. He can't quite manage it so crosses one porky leg over the other still managing to hold onto his breakfast.

'Any exciting plans for today Rupert?'

'No, not really.' He shoves the other half of his bacon sandwich into his mouth. 'Need to have a word with Ralph about the missing woman story.'

He looks in the direction of the Editor's closed office door. Ralph gets in at seven thirty but we all know better than to disturb him before nine o'clock. Smoke drifts into the office from under Ralph's door, he needs at least three cigarettes before he's worth speaking to. No smoking ban for him, he owns the paper as well as being editor so can pretty much do as he likes.

Lucy and Ian arrive by the skin of their teeth at two minutes to nine ready to take their seats before Ralph emerges. At nine on the dot Ralph's door is flung open and he appears in a blast of cigarette smoke.

'Morning, morning, morning,' he says, rubbing his hands together briskly; he's lost without a cigarette in his hand.

'Morning,' we all chorus.

Rupert unwedges himself from his chair and gets up and hands Ralph a sheet of paper, 'This is for tonight's edition, what do you think? Nothing new to write but it's going to be on Crimewatch so we want people to watch it, maybe it'll jog someone's memory.'

Ralph squints at the paper and starts to read,

. . . *Suzanne Jenkins, 45, has now been missing for two weeks. The last sighting of her was at 5pm on 28th April when she left work for the day. Her friends and family say that Ms Jenkins does not have a boyfriend and it is out of character for her to not contact her family. Tonight's 'Crimewatch' is going to stage a reconstruction and if anyone has any information please contact the Frogham police on . . .*

'Yeah, that'll do, Rupe. Not much more you can say, really. She's probably dead anyway.' He gives the paper back to Rupert.

'Christ.' Ian looks up from his desk. 'Talk about look on the dark side, she's only been missing for two weeks'.

'Na, she's dead,' says Ralph confidently. 'Why would she disappear for two weeks? Where would she go – a woman her age? You don't vanish with the clothes you're standing up in and turn up alive'.

I look at the picture of Suzanne Jenkins on my PC, a pretty blond raising a glass of wine to the camera; I have a nagging feeling that I've seen her before. She's the same age as me but I don't think I know her, yet there's something familiar about her. Probably seen her in Asda.

A missing woman is big news for Frogham; nothing much ever happens here. A scrubby patchwork of red brick Victorian terraces, a few streets of posh thirties villas and several estates of sixties square boxes; that pretty much sums up Frogham. Apparently, we have one of the lowest crime rates in the country and it's one of the safest places to live. If the worst has happened to Suzanne Jenkins that'll screw the statistics.

'Let's hope Crimewatch turns something up, though I'm not hopeful,' Ralph goes on. 'Bit sad really, woman of her age. On her own, no husband, no kids, no-one to miss her.'

We're interrupted by the bang of the office door as it's flung open and hits the wall. Lev from the print room appears in the doorway, stomps over to my desk and slaps a sheet of paper down on the desk.

'Is bill, for fix press,' he says, then turns to Ralph. 'Is my neighbour.'

Ralph looks at him blankly.

'My neighbour missing woman. My neighbour.' He points to his chest to make sure we understand.

'Really?' Ralph is shocked, how could he not have known this?

'Yes, she live in up flat.' He points to the ceiling.

Ralph pulls out a chair. 'Sit down, Lev, sit down.' He waves an arm at the seat, the unmistakable scent of a scoop in his nostrils, right here in his own office. Lev lowers himself hesitantly into the seat looking at Ralph suspiciously.

'So.' Ralph claps Lev on the back. 'You say she lives in the flat above you?'

'Is right.'

'How long has she lived there?'

'Politzi say five years but I not know she live there until they question me.

'So, you didn't know her then?'

'No. Not met her but is very sad.' Lev affects a mournful expression.

'You must have seen her about though?'

'No.'

'What, never?'

'No. Dagmar not like me look at other woman. She jealous.'

'Oh. Does Dagmar know her?'

'Not really.'

'What d'you mean, not really?'

4

'She know her but Dagmar no like her, Dagmar say she look like trollop.'

'Trollop? That's not very nice, Lev.'

'I know.' Lev shakes his head. 'Yellow hair and lipstick say trollop to Dagmar, she proper wife.'

'Oh, alright.' Ralph gives Lev one of his looks. 'Let's just hope they catch him and lock him up and throw away the key. Trollop or not.'

'In my country is more simples. We torture him, he confess, we shoot him. Job done, as you say.' Lev shakes his head in disbelief. 'You English, very strange. Prison like holiday camp, colour television. Life of Murphy, as you say.'

'Riley.' says Ralph.

Lev gives Ralph a puzzled look.

'Anyway Lev.' Ralph practically pulls Lev out of the chair. 'Much as I'd like to chat all day I've got work to do.' He puts his hand on Lev's back and gives him a little shove and Lev takes the hint and stomps across the office and back downstairs to the print room.

I'm not really sure where Lev comes from but I'm pretty sure I wouldn't like to live there. I find him a bit intimidating, all swarthy, dark and brooding, but not in a Poldark way. I'm quite relieved he's gone to be honest.

'Bit unfair, calling her a trollop.' Lucy's indignant. 'If dying your hair and wearing lipstick means you're a trollop then so am I.'

'Take no notice, Lucy, if you'd seen Dagmar you'd understand.'

'What do you mean?'

'Well, let's just say,' Ralph goes on, 'that a Russian shot putter and Dagmar have a lot in common. Can someone get that?'

Ralph's phone is ringing from his office. Everyone pretends not to hear it even though it rings and rings.

'I'll get that shall I?' I say sarcastically as I press 0 and pick up the receiver.

'Good morning. Frogham Herald.'

The voice is so faint I can't hear what they're saying, 'Good morning, Frogham Herald.' I say a bit louder.

'Hello, is that the newspaper?' The voice is barely more than a whisper.

'Yes, it's the Frogham Herald, how can I help?' For God's sake get on with it.

'I know who took her. I know who took that woman.'

'You know who took Suzanne Jenkins?' I urge.

Everyone turns to me open mouthed as I listen to the caller; you could hear a pin drop. I listen carefully but the call is brief and after I've put the receiver down I look up to see four pairs of eyes fixed on me. I'm immediately bombarded with questions which I stop by putting my hand up.

'Don't speak to me, I need to write it down.'

I scribble in my notebook as fast I can before I forget what she said. It doesn't take too long and when I've finished I read through it again to make sure I haven't missed anything.

'Okay, all done now.' I say.

'So, come on, spill,' says Ralph impatiently.

I spill. For once Ralph and Ian are in agreement that it's obviously a nutcase. I can tell that Ralph is annoyed that he didn't take the call himself. The fact that the caller has a Scottish accent seems to clinch it.

'Why would they have a Scottish accent?' says

Ralph. 'This is Frogham.' When I point out that Ralph himself comes from London Ian butts in and asks if I'm sure they were Scottish and not Irish.

'I can tell the difference between an Irish and a Scottish accent.' I say witheringly. 'And perhaps if one of you answered the phone now and then you would have spoken to her yourself.'

I've had enough of talking about it now and also the assumption that if they'd answered the phone instead of me they'd have got a lot more information out of her. That'll teach them – perhaps one of them will pick the phone up in future instead of me.

To shut them all up I telephone the police station to report it. I'm sure I'm wasting their time but I can hardly ignore it. I'm put through to the incident team and read the conversation out to them and after I've finished speaking I'm abruptly put on hold. I sit there tapping my fingers for what seems like forever. I'm taken off hold and a different voice informs me that a police officer will be out to visit me within the next hour. I'm really surprised that they're taking this so seriously and feel a twinge of guilt when they tell me not to discuss it with anyone. I've assured them that I won't even though we've done nothing but talk about it for the last hour.

'Right,' I announce, putting down the phone. 'The police are on the way and you have to pretend I haven't told you anything so that I don't look like a complete blabbermouth'.

Excitement over, everyone returns to their desks and Ralph slopes off to his office for a smoke before the police arrive. I just wish the police would hurry up and get here and get it over with.

I'm feeling guilty and I haven't even done

anything.

And I'm feeling anxious.

Very anxious.

The police have arrived – a twelve-year-old detective constable and an older man who introduces himself as Detective Inspector Peters. He's not very policeman like – late 40s, quite tall, with the look of a slightly podgy, greying, Bryan Ferry about him. I feel my face flushing beetroot red because I've met Detective Inspector Peters before, although he doesn't acknowledge that fact to me, or I to him. I'm grateful that he doesn't remember me, or if he does that he pretends not to. I've changed my name since then and I look quite a bit different so I'm hoping that he doesn't remember. He showed me kindness when I probably didn't deserve it and everyone else treated me like a leper.

The three of us go into the kitchen away from the flapping ears of Ralph, Rupert, Ian and Lucy. Ian attempts to follow us through the door muttering something about coffee and tea but I just ignore him and shut the door gently, but firmly, in his face, his nose practically squashed against the glass in the door.

I'd tidied up a bit before they got here –wiped the crumbs off the table and opened the window as there was an odd smell as if something had gone off in the fridge. It's not much of a kitchen, a battered stainless-steel sink and stained worktop with a rusting fridge underneath. They both refuse my offer of a drink which is a relief as I'd be hard pushed to find two cups without chips or disgusting brown stains. We sit down around the table and after the formalities of names we get down to business. My face feels as it's returning to a normal colour.

'So, Ms Russell, can you tell me exactly what she said?'

I pass him the sheet I've typed up. 'I've written it down almost verbatim, as best I can remember.'

'Ah good.' He nods approvingly, them reads through it slowly before passing it to the twelve-year-old.

Me: Good morning. Frogham Herald

Me: Good morning. Frogham Herald

Caller: Hello, is that the newspaper?

Me: Yes, it's the Frogham Herald, how can I help?

Caller: I know who took her. I know who took that woman,

Me: Can you give me your name?

Caller: I can't.

Silence

Caller: I found her bracelet.

Me: Whose bracelet?

Caller: The missing woman's. It has her name on it. Turquoise

beads spelling out her name. He doesn't know I found it.

Me: Who is he? Can you tell me his name?

Caller: I have to go, he's coming... she hangs up.

'How would you say she sounded? Old? Young? nervous?'

'Not a young girl, definitely a woman – and she had a Scottish accent.'

'You're sure she was Scottish? The telephone can be quite distorting.'

'It was definitely a Scottish accent but I don't think she was Scottish.'

'What do you mean? I thought you said she was Scottish?'

'No, she had a Scottish accent but I don't think

she was Scottish. I have a good ear for accents, I think she was trying to disguise her voice. And she sounded frightened.'

'How did she sound frightened?'

'The way she spoke – she was whispering, as if she was afraid someone would hear her, and her voice was a bit wobbly.'

Everything I say is analysed, every detail noted. I can't believe we can talk in such detail about such a brief conversation. He tells me that they have received hundreds of telephone calls and none of them have mentioned the bracelet. This is one of the facts that hasn't been made public, Suzanne Jenkins always wore a beaded name bracelet that her parents had given her for her birthday.

'It could be someone who knows her and knows she has the bracelet and is just ringing up wasting our time,' says Detective Inspector Peters.

'Would someone really do that? Are people really that horrible?' I can hardly believe it.

'I'm afraid they are,' he says with a sigh. 'There really is no limit to how horrible some people are.'

Does he mean me? Does he remember me? I can feel myself starting to blush again. I know I'm paranoid but that doesn't stop my face being on fire. 'This could be a breakthrough,' he continues. 'Or it could be nothing, could just be a timewaster. The big question is what to do next – do we get the newspaper to appeal to the woman to come forward or could that frighten her away or even put her in danger? Also, why did she ring the newspaper and not the incident line?'

He's not asking me, he's talking to himself. I sneak a glance at the twelve-year-old who's surreptitiously flicking through his phone under the table.

'Do you want to put that phone away, Simmons?' The Inspector says drily without even looking at him. The twelve-year-old blushes scarlet and quickly shoves the phone in his trouser pocket. The kitchen must be on fire with the heat from our two faces.

I'm unsure whether I can go or not as the Inspector seems to be in a world of his own. I've also seen Ian and Ralph through the glass in the door walking past several times so I know they're desperate to find out what's being said. I have a little smirk to myself, that'll teach them to pick the phone up in future.

'I think the first thing we need to do is set up a recorder on the phone line here, so if she does ring again we'll have it on tape.'

I nod seriously to show I agree with him but really, I just want this meeting to end so I can go back to my desk and hide.

Before he remembers who I am.

'Yes. I think that's what we'll do.' He stands up then turns to me. 'You've been very helpful Ms Russell and I'm afraid you're going to have to bear with us for a while longer.'

I'm not sure what I'm supposed to say so I nod seriously again and follow him and Simmons out of the tea room.

The next three hours involve a lot of standing around while various police techie types arrive and do things with the telephones. For some reason it's been decided that I will have the recorder on my phone which means I'll be lumbered with all incoming calls. When the techies are satisfied that the voice activated recorder is working they finally leave.

I'm glad to get home. After all the excitement this morning, the afternoon turned into a big rush and it was hard slog to catch up on all my work. Also, the phone never stopped ringing either but the Scottish lady never rang back.

I pull up outside my house and parallel park my car badly in the street. I love my little old terraced house but I hate parallel parking, no matter how much practice I have I just can't master it.

Before I pick up my dog from Linda's I decide to go in and get changed. Sprocket goes to Linda's every day when I'm at work, which he loves as he has Linda's dog, Henry, to keep him company. Linda's house is only two streets away from my own house and what started as a business arrangement has turned into a strong friendship. I quickly run upstairs and change into jeans and t-shirt. As I open the front door to go out again I nearly fall over my brother, Nick, who has his finger poised to press the bell.

'Hello you,' he says, wrapping his arms around me in a bear hug as he comes in.

I let myself be hugged. 'Hello yourself. I didn't know you were coming - you never said.'

'Well, I hadn't planned to, but to be honest I'm a bit worried about Dad. And anyway,' he says, 'I was on a promise with a model from Mayfair but she's getting a bit serious so I thought I'd make myself scarce.'

'Did you tell her you wouldn't be seeing her?'

'Ummm. Might have forgotten to...' he says with a sheepish smile.

'God, Nick you're such a shit.'

'I know.' He laughs.

I've just closed the door when the doorbell rings again and this time it's Linda with Sprocket. I immediately feel guilty as she does so much for me and I should have gone and got him straight away. Sprocket comes bounding through the door towards me then sees Nick so veers towards him and launches himself at Nick's knees. He jumps around, ears flapping, and whimpering until he gets some attention.

'Just remember who feeds you, dog,' I say. Sprocket ignores me and rolls over onto his back so Nick can kneel down and rub his tummy. Linda steps past Nick and hands me Sprocket's lead.

'Hey, Nick, meet Linda, Linda, meet Nick, my brother.'

'Ah, so you're the dog-lady,' says Nick with his most charming smile. He offers his hand.

This is when the 'Nick effect' usually happens and most women turn into simpering messes. He's a bit of a looker my brother. Open any upmarket, glossy magazine and chances are that the handsome man advertising aftershave or suits is my brother.

So, with something like boredom I wait for the simpering to begin.

And then the strangest thing happens.

The Nick effect doesn't work, at all. It's a complete fail.

'Hello Nick,' says Linda coldly, shaking Nick's hand 'Nice to meet you.'

I can tell this has taken the wind out of his sails; he's not used to this non-reaction. He tries again. 'Have we....'

Linda has already turned her back on him to speak to me and totally ignores him. 'I'm going out so I thought I'd drop Sprocket off, must dash but I'll catch up with you tomorrow.' And with that she's out of the door and gone.

'Well, that was awkward,' says a very put out Nick. 'Do you think it's because I called her dog-lady?'

I think about it for a moment. 'No, I don't think so, she wouldn't care about that.' I know that she wouldn't. 'Not *everyone* has to fancy you, you know.' I can't help laughing at his crestfallen face. 'Welcome to the real world. That's what it's like for the rest of us most of the time, you're just not used to it.'

'Hmm, do you think I'm losing my looks? I mean, I am forty-two.'

'Of course you're not. You know you look as good as ever so stop fishing for compliments.'

'No, you're right.' He puffs his chest out. 'Is she gay?'

Chapter Two

'Come on Sprocket don't sulk.'

Sprocket looks at the treat I'm offering him with disgust then turns his head without taking it and puts his nose in the air. He always knows when I'm leaving him on his own. We're going out and he's seen me putting his favourite toy rabbit out of his reach. If I don't do this its ears will be gone when I come back. I really can't be bothered to cook, so Nick and I are going to call into the Swan for something to eat on the way to Dad's.

Leaving behind a very disgruntled Sprocket, Nick and I arrive at the Swan, our local gastro pub. There are people outside in the garden although they're mostly smokers as it's not *that* warm. It's busy – Thursday night is quiz night – but we manage to get a very small table for two in the corner. Heads turn as we walk through the bar and I get the usual *what's he doing with her* looks from other women. Nick and I don't look alike so people assume I'm his girlfriend; I like to think that I'm okay looking but I'm definitely not in my brother's league. I'm used to it now but sometimes I just wish someone would look at *me*.

We manoeuvre ourselves into our seats and give the waitress our order; she's dismissive of me but hangs on Nick's every word. I am trying to lose some weight and had intended ordering salad but one whiff of the smell from the kitchen and that resolve flies out of the window. We order steak and chips and in no time, are tucking into them. Nick is back to his normal chirpy self now that he's been reassured that he hasn't lost his looks overnight. The waitress hovers and asks if the food is okay. I have to shove another chip in my mouth to stop myself from shouting *HE'S MY BROTHER* at her to wipe away the filthy look she's directing at me. Nick gives her a beaming smile and assures her that the food is *just wonderful, thank you.* Bit much, it's not that good but he can't help turning on the charm.

'So,' says Nick, 'this Linda – got a girlfriend or boyfriend, has she?'

'No, she hasn't got a boyfriend and she's not gay as far as I know.'

'Hmm....'

'Don't you dare, Nick.'

'What?' he says, affecting innocence.

'Don't you dare make it your mission to seduce her. Leave her alone. She's my friend.'

Nick smiles smugly.

'I won't.'

'I don't believe you, I know what you're like.'

Nick puts his hands up in defence, 'I won't – scout's honour.'

'You'd better not Nick.' I say firmly and maybe a little aggressively.

'Can I get you more drinks?' The over attentive waitress is back, simpering at my brother. She's just reapplied fresh lipstick for his benefit and it's all over her front teeth.

'No, I'm good thanks.'

She flutters her eyelashes at him and turns to walk

away.

'I'd like one,' I say loudly.

She turns back unsmiling and raises an eyebrow at me, pencil poised over notepad.

'Diet coke, please.'

She writes it down and turns to walk away without acknowledging me.

'Oh, and by the way,' I say spitefully, 'you've got lipstick all over your teeth.'

She pauses without turning, then walks away.

'Christ, you're in a brutal mood tonight,' Nick says when she's gone. 'What's she ever done to you?'

'Ignored me,' I snap. 'Which you could never understand because it's never happened to you. Oh, until Linda . . .' I start to laugh.

'So,' Nick, putting his pint down carefully, doesn't bite. 'Do you want to tell me what's really bothering you?'

We arrive at Dad's, he still lives in the house we grew up in; a seventies time warp of swirly patterned carpets, clashing flowery curtains and dust gathering ornaments. It's far too big for an old man on his own but Dad would never consider moving into anything smaller, not voluntarily anyway. The back garden is humungous, I think whoever built the house did a deal with the builder as it not only has a long garden but also has a sort of T-junction at the end that runs along the back of everyone else's gardens. Dad's neighbour, Simon, is an Estate agent and is always telling Dad he could make a fortune if he sold some of the garden off, but Dad won't hear of it.

I ring the bell and Dad opens the door in his *casual* wear, which is basically a suit and tie minus the jacket.

'Hello,' he says unenthusiastically. 'You'd better come in.'

'Hello Dad,' Nick and I trill as we go in. 'How are you?'

'Oh, you know, mustn't complain.' He says, then launches into a lengthy moan. Nick settles himself on the sofa and buries his nose in the evening paper. He'll make the odd grunt or word of acknowledge to pretend he's listening but will leave me to do the talking.

Dad's moaning about the *new* next-door neighbour who moved in six months ago. I don't know why but he has taken such an instant dislike to him. As far as I know the man has done nothing to upset Dad – he came round and introduced himself and by all accounts was pleasant enough but for some reason Dad can't stand him. He doesn't even like his name. 'Brendan! What sort of a name is Brendan?' Poor bloke can do nothing right.

'He starts that car up at all times of the day and night.'

'It's a taxi, Dad.'

'Well, it wakes me up and I can't get back to sleep. I can hear him start it up and the headlights shine right into my bedroom.' I can believe the lights wake him up but not the noise – Dad struggles to hear what I say even when I shout.

'I don't know how it can wake you up when you're deaf.'

'What did you say? You're mumbling.'

Like I say, he's taken a dislike to him. Dad's deaf in both ears and has his television on so loud that it's impossible to speak over it let alone hear a car start up outside. And when he goes to bed he takes his hearing aids out.

'I don't see how he can afford a house like that on his own, he must be up to no good. He's bringing the neighbourhood down. Taxi driver indeed.'

Built in the fifties, the houses in Dad's street were for the middle classes, individually designed with at least four bedrooms and giant gardens. He's right – you would need a very good job or a medium sized lottery win to afford a house in this street now. Brendan must do a lot of taxi runs.

'What no good is he up to Dad?'

Dad ponders the question for a while then gives a wry smile.

'I don't know, but he's up to something, you wait and see.'

We both laugh and to get him off the subject of the neighbour I ask him if he's been to his gardening club today – he hasn't and says he can't be bothered with it. He hasn't been for a few weeks now but he is seventy-nine so I think he's allowed not to be bothered if he feels like it. I suggest, again, that maybe we could get someone in to help with the garden as it's overgrown and very large.

Dad harrumphs. 'Nosey parkers and interfering people,' he mutters.

So I let it go. It's like a jungle at the bottom of the garden but it's not as if it's affecting anyone else.

'He was in my garden you know.' He's back on the Brendan subject again.

'Who?'

'Him. Next door. Brendan,' he snorts. 'I looked out of the kitchen window and there he was, bold as brass. Thought I couldn't see him he did, he thinks I'm senile you know but I'm not daft. It might have been getting dark but I saw him alright. He was lurking down the bottom by my shed. Up to no good. '

'But how could he get in your garden?' I shout. 'You always keep the side gate locked.'

The shed down the end is full of old lawnmowers and tools. It's been locked for years and never gets used anymore although it was great when we were kids, we'd put all the tools up one end of the shed and use the rest as our den.

'ISN'T THAT RIGHT? NICK.' I shout louder.

'What?' Nick looks at me blankly.

'Dad's just saying that Brendan was in his garden but he couldn't be, could he?' I glare at Nick and he takes the hint and puts the newspaper down.

'Lou's right Dad, your garden is intruder proof, so you don't need to worry.

'I'm telling you he does. I don't know how he gets in but somehow, he does. I'm not going to stand for it much more.' He gets up from his chair and wags his finger at Nick. 'Something will have to be done.'

Neither Nick nor I say anything.

'I'm going to make some tea.' He plods out to the kitchen.

Nick and I exchange meaningful glances as we listen to Dad rattling cups and clattering around the kitchen. There have been quite a few episodes lately of Dad thinking people were here when they weren't. I've come round after work and Dad has been convinced that I'd already visited earlier in the day. He's been the same with Nick. We've told Dad that he must have fallen asleep and been dreaming that we were here but I think we were trying to convince ourselves more than him. He's also got lost quite a few times on the way back from the shops – a journey he must have done a million times. I feel suddenly deflated and unaccountably sad and realise I have no control over anything. I look at Nick and he smiles a tight-lipped smile. We're kidding ourselves and trying to delay the inevitable, but we both know Dad's not right and hasn't been for a long time.

Dad reappears with two mugs of tea and puts mine down next to me and offers Nick his.

'You were a bit rude yesterday, weren't you?' Dad says as Nick takes the tea from him.

'Eh? What? I never saw you yesterday.'

'Coming in here', Dad continues as if Nick hasn't spoken. 'Sitting there, reading my paper then just leaving without a word when I go into the kitchen to make some tea. I brought you up better than that, Nicholas.'

Nick and I exchange surreptitious glances, another phantom visit.

'Oh, yeah, sorry Dad, was in a bit of a hurry, late for a meeting, you know. I did call out bye but you couldn't have heard me'.

Dad says nothing but looks slightly mollified; although he's as deaf as a post he won't admit it, says we all need to learn to speak properly.

I feel guilty that I can't be here all of the time. Mum died five years ago and, to be honest, I thought Dad wouldn't be far behind her but somehow, he's kept going on his own even though he misses her like mad. Mum and Dad were inseparable and I can honestly say I never heard them argue. Truly. Mum lived in a state of constant anxiety and worried about everything – if we were late home from school she thought we'd been abducted and a cold was always a life-threatening illness. Her whole life was lived in a state of waiting for something terrible to happen. Not much sympathy from other people over mental health problems then – you were just supposed to get on with and stop making such a meal of it. Nowadays, there would be help of course, counselling maybe, but then there was nothing – just my dad. It must have been really hard for them - no brothers or sisters and both of their parents dead before I was even born. I can't imagine what it'd be like not having a brother. Annoying though he is.

We drink our tea and make the usual chit chat then Dad engrosses himself reading the classified ads in the Herald with the help of a magnifying glass. I gather up my coat and handbag and lean down and kiss Dad on the cheek.

'We've got to get off now, Dad. Don't forget Jean is coming tomorrow. I've written it on your calendar.'

Jean comes in every weekday to Dad's for three hours; she cleans, cooks him a bit of dinner and has a chat to him. She's been coming a few months now and at first he put up a bit of a fight and said he didn't need looking after, but I think he quite enjoys the company now.

'Okay. Drive carefully.' He always, *always*, says that.

Sprocket has forgiven me for abandoning him earlier and we snuggle on the sofa to watch TV. Nick has left for London as he's got a shoot in the morning. We're in a quandary about Dad; we know that there's something wrong with him but haven't a clue what to do about it. I can't see Dad agreeing to go to the doctors but I think we definitely need to stop him driving. Even if we can persuade him to seek medical help, what happens then? There's no magic pill.

I've recorded Crimewatch so I can watch the reconstruction. There's not a lot to it, a five-minute segment of Suzanne walking from her office in town to her car. Her car is still parked in the car park where she left it the morning she disappeared. Watching it, I'm struck by how close her workplace is to mine; that's probably where I've seen her.

Sprocket is fast asleep and his feet are twitching so he must be dreaming of chasing rabbits. I never thought I would have a dog, but then I never thought after twenty years of marriage my husband would leave me for someone half my age. I wouldn't have Sprocket if I was still married to Gerry, he was allergic to fur so I was banned from having a pet. Not his fault I know, but I think it was just a bit too convenient him being allergic as he didn't like animals.

'Don't see the point of animals.' His words still ring in my ears. Unless he was eating them.

Sprocket's a mixture of breeds. There's a fair bit of spaniel in him and he's quite furry and has floppy ears but I'm hard pushed to pick out any other breeds. Nick appeared with him one day when I was at my lowest. A Saturday lunchtime and I was still slobbing around in my dressing gown and feeling sorry for myself. Nick arrived unannounced with a tiny bundle of fur, and thrust him at me.

'You always wanted a dog when we were kids,' he said, handing him to me. 'So here you are.' I was annoyed and told him I didn't want the bother of a dog, but Nick just ignored me.

'It'll do you good, give you something to do, take it

23

for a walk, brush its fur or whatever it is you do with a dog.'

'Hasn't it got a name?' I asked Nick sulkily.

'Not yet. Call it after your ex if you can't think of anything else.'

'What, Gerry?'

'I was thinking more of Tosser or Dickhead.'

In the end I decided on Sprocket because I just liked the sound of it. Sprocket did too because he answered to it the first time I called him. So that's how I came to have a dog and it sounds dramatic but I think Sprocket saved me – he made me get up and get out in the fresh air and stop being so self-pitying. I'd like to say that he's taken an instant dislike to Gerry on the rare occasions he's been in his company but unfortunately Sprocket is a complete traitor dog and loves everyone. He does make Gerry sneeze though, so I have to be grateful for that.

Sprocket's better company than Gerry. He doesn't whinge or prattle on about his oh so important job and he's happy to watch whatever I want on telly too. I sometimes wonder how Gerry's new young wife is finding her much older husband and how her much older husband is enjoying life with his very young wife and young family.

Gerry and I were married for twenty years and we were happy enough, we rarely argued and had a good life together. We agreed early in our marriage that we didn't want children, or maybe Gerry decided and I just agreed with him – I tended to do that. We had a lovely home and money wasn't a problem and we always had nice holidays and doesn't that just sound completely dull and boring? We met when we both worked in the same office although Gerry was swiftly promoted and is now a director whereas I was quite happy as an accountant. When I think back now, our marriage had probably run its course as we were more like friends than lovers and if he hadn't been so spineless and devious it would probably have been an amicable split.

I remember the night it all went wrong – the divorce was going through and Gerry had moved into a flat while our lovely house was up for sale. He'd insisted that there was no one else involved and although I had my suspicions I decided it was easier just to believe him; it was less painful that way, less humiliating. The company Christmas dinner dance was being held at a plush hotel just outside town. I'd dropped quite a bit of weight without even trying due to the divorce-diet and I was wearing a slinky black number with killer heels and I felt pretty good. I didn't have much of an appetite so left most of my meal but drank glass after glass of wine and couldn't seem to stop. Loud and obnoxious that was me, basically just showing off. If Gerry hadn't been there I would've probably fallen asleep, been helped into a taxi and gone home.

I don't remember a lot of it, just snapshots of me cavorting around on the dance floor and going to the toilets to constantly spray myself with perfume and reapply lipstick until I looked like the joker with jammy red lips. I cringe just thinking about it and unfortunately, I've seen the photos on Facebook to prove how truly awful I looked.

In my drunken stupor I think I was trying to show Gerry what he was missing even though I didn't want him anymore. He was sitting with the other directors and their wives who had once been my friends, too. I was strutting past him to go to the toilets yet again when I saw his secretary, who was standing behind him, lean down to talk to him, and it was the way he looked at her, I just *knew*. He used to look at me like that and I knew in that instant that there was someone else and it was her. How could I have been so dim and not have known? She was young, extremely pretty and it was just such a cliché and I felt a complete idiot. All the sympathetic looks directed my way suddenly made sense, obviously everyone knew except for me.

I carried on walking to the toilets only this time I didn't bother applying more lipstick and when I came tottering back I was holding a big filthy mop that I'd found in the cleaners' cupboard. I remember Gerry's lopsided smile that I'd always loved but now find so irritating, the disgusting smell of the mop, Gerry's smile turning to horror as he saw me approaching. He shouted at me to stop being ridiculous and calm down – telling someone to calm down never works does it? I can't recall my exact words as I shoved the mop straight at his face but it was something along the lines of 'you fucking cheating bastard'.

I try not to think about the rest of that night as it only got worse and I actually got arrested and spent the night sleeping it off in a police cell. I could have avoided being arrested if I'd agreed to be taken home but I wouldn't; I created such a scene and wouldn't shut up so they had no choice but to arrest me. I never have known when to shut up.

Detective Inspector Peters happened to be at the station when I arrived, luckily for me. The arresting PC was sick to death of me and my arguing by then and if DI Peters hadn't stepped in and defused the situation I think I would have been charged. He arranged for gallons of black coffee to be given to me and tried to talk some sense into me. The shame of waking up the next morning in a cell still makes me break out in a sweat.

So, I never went back to Bracewells, not even to clear my desk out. They graciously put me on gardening leave then made me redundant, which Gerry probably instigated. I would have left anyway, there's no way I could have gone back, I felt too ashamed.

Gerry's married to her now and of course like most twenty-somethings she wanted the lovely house with two lovely children. Well she has the lovely house and the two children though on the occasions that I've bumped into them they're always screaming and definitely not lovely. Gerry always looks completely frazzled. She made it her mission to update Gerry and he quickly dropped a couple of stone and took up cycling to keep trim. He may be slim and toned but to me he just looks grey and thin. I prefer a bit of chub myself especially as you get older. Poor Gerry, 49 with two children under 3, sounds like a nightmare. That's the trouble with marrying someone so much younger – they just make you look old and knackered.

Anyway, we're civil to each other, although now the finances are sorted there is absolutely no reason to ever see him again.

I wish him well.

The prick.

Sprocket snuggles into my neck and gazes up at me adoringly and gives a big sigh. I know he's spotted the chocolate biscuit left on my plate and is hoping

I'll give it to him. I decide I'll have to eat it so he can't.

'Sorry but you can't have it or you'll be a dead dog,' I say as I cram it into my mouth. Sprocket frowns at me and then suddenly his head jerks up and he emits a low growl – this means the phone is about to ring. I don't know how he knows but he always does. On cue the phone rings and I look at the clock, it's half past ten and I know it must be Dad as he's probably the only person in the world who doesn't text or WhatsApp me.

I pick the phone up, 'Hello,' I mumble through the biscuit.

'Hello. Is that Louise.'

'YES, IT'S ME DAD,' I shout.

'Is it? It doesn't sound like Louise. Are you sure?'

'YES, I'M SURE,' I shout louder. We go through this palaver every time he rings and I often end up just going round to his house to find out what he wants. It's easier than shouting myself hoarse.

'What's the matter Dad?'

'It's him,' he whispers.

'You'll have to speak up Dad I can hardly hear you.'

'I don't want him to hear,' he says a bit louder. 'It's him next door. He's done it again. I'm going to call the cops.'

Call the cops? My dad doesn't say *call the cops*. Why is he talking like that?

'It's okay dad. I'll come round, don't worry I won't be long.'

'NO! You can't, it's not safe. He's in my garden, I've seen him...I can hear him, he's taunting me, he's laughing at me. I'm going to get my air gun and see him off...'

'No, don't Dad. Stay indoors and keep the door locked and I'll come round. I'll bring Sprocket with me, he'll scare him off." A vision of my dad careering round the street with an air gun pops into my head. God, it doesn't bear thinking about. With a lot of cajoling I manage to calm him down and get him to promise me he'll stay indoors until I get there. I quickly throw my jacket on, grab my keys and pick up Sprocket's dog lead – I daren't let him loose in Dad's garden or I'll never find him again.

'Come on Sprocket, time to get your harness on.'

Sprawled on the sofa with his paws in the air, Sprocket yawns and looks up at me.

Guard dog, indeed.

Chapter Three

I can hear a bell ringing and it won't stop.

It's the alarm. I reach out to silence it, unable to believe it's time to get up. Typically, I tossed and turned all night after my visit to Dad but half an hour ago I went into a deep and lovely sleep. Sprocket is a dead weight on my feet and showing no sign of moving. I reach my hand down to him to make sure he's still breathing – he's sleeps so soundly without moving that I sometimes wake in the middle of the night and put the light on to make sure he's not dead.

Last night. After Dad's panicked phone call, I drove over to his house. What's normally a fifteen-minute drive took me less than ten as I put my foot down, worried what I was going to find when I got there.

The house was in darkness. I tried to open the front door with my key but Dad had dead locked it and I couldn't get it open, not without a lump hammer. I then spent ten minutes banging the door knocker, ringing the bell and phoning him from my mobile. All sorts of things were running through my head – was he wandering the streets with his air gun? Was he dead? I was just about to give up and go and ask Simon next door to help me break in when the door was yanked open by Dad. With an extremely annoyed look on his face.

'What are you doing here? It's late you know. I was just going to bed.'

'You rang me,' I shouted loudly, aware that he didn't have his hearing aids in.

He looked at me as if I was mad then begrudgingly said, 'Come in.' He glared at Sprocket and said, 'I suppose you'd better bring that in as well.'

'YOU RANG ME,' I shouted once we were inside the house.

'Rang you? Why would I ring you?'

He looked genuinely puzzled, his hair sticking up in fluffy tufts and his pyjamas buttoned up on the wrong buttons. I felt a rush of protective love for him. He looked so vulnerable. So old.

He didn't remember ringing me at all although it was less than half an hour previously. We then had a surreal conversation where I tried to convince him that he really had phoned me and that I wasn't mistaken. I gave up in the end and made a cup of tea while Dad followed Sprocket around the lounge telling him not to touch anything. It obviously didn't work as I found a china rabbit of Dad's in his basket this morning next to my television remote control.

While I was in Dad's kitchen waiting for the kettle to boil I unlocked the back door for a look in the garden. I walked out a little way from the house shining my phone torch in front of me. It was so dark out there that only a tiny patch in front of me was lit and my imagination started wondering what was in the bits that I couldn't see. I didn't like it one bit and hastily went back into the kitchen and closed and locked the door. I shut his kitchen blinds as well as I had the horrible feeling that if I looked out I might see someone looking right back at me. Paranoia, I told myself.

I don't think I could live there on my own.

I finally got home after midnight and Dad seemed fine when I left him although he still didn't remember ringing me, at all. He almost convinced me that I'd imagined it. Perhaps I'm the one going doolally.

Work seems never ending, the dullest Friday morning ever, not helped by the fact that I have to answer every phone call as I have the listening equipment on my phone. The *Scottish* lady doesn't ring and I feel disgruntled and irritable that I've got stuck with answering the phone all the time as well as all of my other work.

The sun is shining through the window and when I look down into the precinct I can see people in t-shirts and summer dresses and there's even a few with shorts on. At lunchtime I grab my bag and wander down into the square to enjoy the sunshine and eat my sandwiches. I settle myself on a free bench in front of Specsavers, take my mobile out and ring Jean to find out how Dad is.

'He's fine,' says Jean. 'He's been busy sorting out the understairs cupboard – has everything out all over the hallway and wouldn't let me help even though I offered. I think he's quite enjoying himself.' I know she thinks Nick and I are fussing, but she hasn't witnessed any of Dad's episodes. Maybe I am fussing, maybe Dad's fine and it's a normal part of getting old.

'Anyway, dear,' she says, 'there's no need to worry about tomorrow as that nice Mr Harper next door said he'd pop in and have a cup of tea with your Dad.'

I'm relieved that Simon is going to pop in, Dad likes him and his wife, Eileen. I know Simon will let me know if there's a problem. A small, selfish part of me is also pleased that I won't have to interrupt my Saturday to go round there. I'll take him out for Sunday lunch instead. We could go to the Swan; it'll make a nice change for him. Well, he'll probably moan to be honest, but the Swan cooks a better roast than I do.

Saturday morning dawns bright and sunny, unbelievable weather for a weekend. I wait while Linda locks her front door and Sprocket and Henry run around her legs tangling their leads together.

'Not sold yet then?' I nod at the *for sale* sign nailed to next door's garden wall.

'Not as far as I know. Loads of people have looked at it, that slimy estate agent seems to be there every day. Ugh. He's horrible, eyes everywhere when he talks to you, really fancies himself. I hope someone buys it soon. I don't like it being empty.'

'Where did they move to?'

'Nowhere. Was a little old lady on her own, she died and the family are selling it. I'll be glad when it's sold – gives me the creeps.'

'Why?'

'Dunno,' she shrugs, 'it just does. I keep hearing things. Maybe it's haunted.'

I look at Linda to see if she's joking, she's not.

'What sort of things?'

'Creaks, thuds. Footsteps like someone's going up and down the stairs.'

'Well it's an old house, you know how houses make funny noise. It'll be the sudden warm weather, makes the wood dry out.'

Linda doesn't look convinced.

It is warm though, typical British weather, going from frost at night into shorts and flip flop weather in the space of a few days. No doubt next week I'll be back in socks and boots. I have my springy soled flip flops on for the first time this year. I look down at my feet, they look decidedly hoof like and are definitely not summer ready. Certainly lacking in the nail varnish department. Linda has pink doc martins on. Apart from taking her coat off she wears the same summer and winter: black trousers, black t shirt. She has vampire white skin and always sits in the shade so she never gets a tan. I don't think I've ever even seen her sweat. I know by the time we get back from our walk she'll be cool and unruffled and I'll be a clammy mess. She laughs when I joke that I'm afraid she might bite me. And *she's* afraid of noises from next door.

We amble the short walk to the Rise, the distant drone of a lawnmower and a whiff of barbeque in the air. They're starting early, it's only ten o'clock.

We unclip the dogs' leads and Sprocket and Henry gallop off, ears flying. I don't know why it's called the Rise, or to give it it's full name, Frogham Rise. Just a large field with houses backing onto it on three sides, it's not even a slope let alone a hill. Funfairs pitch up here a few times a year and the local radio station does a firework display in November but mostly it's just dog walkers and kids kicking a ball around. As well as the usual dog walker the sunshine has bought out packs of Lycra clad joggers and water bottle holding power walkers.

'Oh shit, there's The Truth. Quick, walk the other way before he sees us,' says Linda out of the corner of her mouth.

Too late, Norman Shuttleworth, more commonly known as *The Truth* due to his finishing most sentences with 'and that's the God's honest truth,' and Frogham's most insufferable bore, has seen us and is marching purposefully towards us dragging his poodle Lulu behind him. Ten minutes in The Truth's company and you feel like throwing yourself under the nearest bus.

'Hellooo.'

'Morning.' We attempt to edge away in the opposite direction.

'Have you heard about....' he starts prattling and walks with us until we give in and stop. Lulu lies down, yawns and closes her eyes for a long sleep.

'We can't really stop,' I shout over him as he launches into his monologue. 'We're just on our way home.'

'...and God's honest truth...' he doesn't even pause for breath and continues talking over us, nothing will stop him, he's started his script and will finish it. I'm sure if a bomb dropped on him his mouth would still go on talking. I can already feel the life being sucked out of me and start to pray that my phone will ring. I wonder if it's possible to ring Linda's mobile from the phone in my pocket.

Pushing fifty, The Truth has thinning sandy hair and wing nut ears. He still lives with his mum who is stone deaf, luckily for her. He often cycles past my house, usually with a crowd of kids behind him shouting, 'Get off and milk it.'

We try edging away again, he follows.

Fifteen minutes later he's still going and I'm starting to feel panicked. We could be here for days at this rate. I'm considering feigning a heart attack or epileptic fit when an unlikely rescuer appears.

'OI YOU!'

We all look around to see a short, square woman waving a plastic bag in the air stomping towards The Truth.

'Yeah, you with the ears.' She yells, shoving the plastic bag at him. 'Clear up your dog shit, mate, or I'll report you.'

Miracle of miracles, he actually stops talking. Lulu wakes up and jumps up then shakily reverses backwards behind The Truth in an attempt to hide.

'I'm, I'm really sorry. I didn't realise, God's honest truth.'

'Yeah, that's what they all say mate. Just shut your gob and clear it up. If I catch you again I'll definitely report you.' She jabs a meaty index finger at him to punctuate every word.

Amazingly, The Truth stops talking and scuttles over to the offending pile and with shaking hands attempts to clean it up with the bag. Square woman stands over him and watches to make sure he does it properly.

Linda and I speed walk away.

'Don't you feel a bit mean?' I say to Linda. 'Do you think we should have stayed and stuck up for him? I don't think it was even his dog that did it.'

'Absolutely not – wish I'd known that it was that easy to shut him up. I might try shouting at him next time.'

'That woman was a bit frightening though – wouldn't want to meet her down a dark alley.'

'Nor me. Which reminds me - do you fancy coming to mine tonight for a barbeque? I've got an old friend coming round for the evening. Haven't seen her for years and to be honest she sort of invited herself. Please say you'll come.' She looks at me pleadingly when I hesitate. 'Bloody Facebook. I wish I'd just ignored her friend request. There's a good reason I haven't seen her for years, we weren't exactly the best of friends.'

'Oh, alright then. She can't be that bad.'

'Trust me, she can. Bring Sprocket as well. She hates animals so we can get Henry and Sprocket to climb all over her and make her leave early.'

'Why didn't you just keep making excuses and she'd get the hint eventually.'

'She won't. If you think The Truth's bad just wait until you meet Glenda.'

I laugh. 'I don't believe you.'

'You'll see. At least the Truth's pleasant, more than I can say for Glenda.'

'I'll be changing my mind in a minute if she's that bad.'

'You wouldn't. Would you?' Linda looks over her shoulder, 'He's finished and on our tail.'

I glance back to see The Truth heading towards us with a plastic bag in his hand, Lulu trotting behind.

We break into a run.

I arrive at Linda's back gate at six-thirty with Sprocket and a bottle of wine. I love Linda's garden, it's small but packed with lots of pots with plants that always seem to be in flower and when the weather's nice you can pretend you're in Spain. Fairy lights and bunting trail along the fence and all of the pots are painted pastel blues and pinks. You can almost forget you're in the back yard of an old two up two down terrace.

I open the gate and let myself in, Linda is barbequing and calls out hello. I'm surprised to see Glenda is already here. I thought I'd get here extra early but she's beaten me to it. She's making no secret of looking me up and down and I don't think she likes what she sees.

'Hello. So, you're Louise.'

'I am,' I say with a smile. 'You must be Glenda. Nice to meet you.'

She sort of sniffs at me so I plonk the wine down on the table and settle down in the chair opposite her, trying to affect an open and friendly expression. She frowns at me so maybe I look more half-wit than amicable. I help myself to a handful of crisps from the table while sending Linda a telepathic message to turn around from the barbeque.

I can tell by the set of Linda's shoulders that she's had enough of Glenda already.

Sprocket bustles over to greet Glenda, tail swishing furiously. Glenda looks down at him with distaste. Sprocket sits next to her gazing at her with *love me* eyes. I know he won't leave her alone until she makes a fuss of him; he thinks everyone has to love him.

'Are these snacks gluten free, Linda?' Glenda asks, looking at the bowls of crisps on the table.

Linda turns around, spatula in hand.

'No, 'fraid not, Glenda. I've got some peanuts though; would they be any good?'

Glenda pulls a face.

'No, I can't eat peanuts. They upset my stomach. IBS.' Glenda pats her stomach.

'Have a glass of wine,' I say. I open the bottle and gather three glasses from the table.

'No thanks. I don't drink, do I?'

'Oh, sorry.' I don't know why I'm apologising. How should I know whether she drinks or not? I'd definitely be deleting her from Facebook if I was Linda.

We sit in uncomfortable silence with the sizzle of the barbeque the only sound. For the life of me I can't think of anything to say and am just about to resort to talking about the weather when Linda turns around.

'I've done hot dogs, burgers and chicken fillets and there's salad and baps on the table. Bring your plates over and tell me what you want.'

'I'll just have a bap and a little salad, Linda. I find my diet is so restrictive what with being gluten free, my IBS and my allergies. There's barely anything I can eat. I exist on practically nothing,' Glenda says piously.

I study Glenda while she's not looking. She's very pretty in a glossy, manicured way which is spoilt only by her petulant mouth. A few more years and that mouth will set in a firm line. I feel ridiculously pleased with myself for painting my toenails and putting on a bit of makeup. Imagine Glenda's horror if she's seen the state of my hooves earlier.

The food smells delicious so I have one of everything. Sprocket has given up on Glenda and is sitting with Henry under the table. They're both drooling and waiting for some barbeque food to come their way. Linda sits herself between me and Glenda and I hope I can eat my food, guzzle some wine and slope off home early.

'Your brother's called Nick, isn't he?'

I almost jump out of my skin, I wasn't expecting Glenda to bother talking to me. She has a dry bap, a lettuce leaf and half a tomato on her plate. I didn't think bread was gluten free, but what do I know?

'He is, do you know him?'

'Yes, Linda and I were at school with him weren't we Linda?'

Linda nods. Well, I never knew that. Nick is a couple of years younger than me so they'd be the same age, but Linda has never mentioned that she knew Nick at school or that she even went to the same school as him, or me. I don't remember Linda from school but being two years older than her she wouldn't have been on my radar – and it was a massive comprehensive school anyway.

'You don't look a bit like him,' Glenda says accusingly, as if it's my fault. 'He was really good looking, wasn't he?'

Well, thanks for that, Glenda.

'He was quite the heart throb at school wasn't he, Linda?' she goes on. 'I remember all the girls used to write his name on their daps, hilarious! I expect he's old, fat and balding now, isn't he?' she says hopefully, nibbling on a lettuce leaf.

'No, he's a model actually.' I sound prissy and annoyed even to my own ears. 'You never mentioned that you knew him, Linda.'

'Well he wouldn't remember *her*, would he?' cuts in Glenda. 'She was the class mouse – I doubt anyone remembers Linda.'

'Wow, Linda you said that without even opening your mouth.' I say sarcastically. Linda's face has gone slightly red.

'Well there's no need to be rude. I just tell it like it is. Your brother was one of the good looking popular ones and Linda was one of the unfortunates. You know, every class had a pretty one, a fat one, a swotty one and a mouse. Linda was the mouse.' She smiles at Linda. 'But you're not a mouse now are you Linda? You're completely different now. I think that's what your weird dress sense is all about – you're determined not to be ignored. Although you can wear what you like, working from home. Doesn't really matter if no one sees you. What was it you said you do? Book editing?'

'Yes.' Linda says, tight lipped.

I'm trying to understand why Linda never told me she knew my brother, I've talked about him often enough. Whichever way I look at it it's strange that she never told me. I won't ask her in front of Glenda though, that's a conversation for another day. Odd though, and she blanked him the other day too.

'Your brother probably remembers me – I actually went out with him for a few weeks in year nine.'

'Oh, I'll be sure to remember you to him,' I say to Glenda. 'I'll bet you haven't changed at all.' She preens when I say this but it's not a compliment. Nick probably went out with every pretty girl in the school, he even went out with my some of my friends and they were two years older than him. I doubt he'll remember Glenda, she was one of many.

'So, Linda, how long has next door been for sale? Only I'm thinking of doing a buy to let and one of these little houses would probably do. I couldn't live in one but I'm sure they'd be easy to rent out to the lower end of the market.'

Well, she insults both of us in one go. No wonder Linda can't stand her. I can't stand her.

'It's only been for sale about a month. Loads of interest though so you'd better get in quick.'

'Mmm. Maybe I'll give the estate agent a ring tomorrow. Be good to put my money somewhere. I mean, there's just nowhere to invest these days that pays a decent return, is there?'

Linda and I murmur agreement. Like we'd know. I'm determined not to ask her where she lives or what she does.

I don't need to.

'The salon in Hope Street has really taken off. It's doing nearly as well as the one in the precinct. Have you ever been in there, Louise?'

Ah, that explains the perfect hair, make-up and line free face. She's *that* Glenda, as in 'Glenda's Beauty' salons. No, I've never been in either of them. Even if I wanted to, I probably couldn't afford to.

'No, I haven't.'

'Thought not. Well, if you ever feel the urge let me know and I'll give you some discount vouchers.'

I resist the urge to tell her where she can stuff her vouchers as she prattles on giving unwanted beauty advice to Linda. I zone out. I'm wondering how soon I can make my escape and get away from this hideous woman. Linda was right, The Truth would be better company than her, as least he's not nasty.

I pour myself and Linda another glass of wine.

It's going to be a long night.

Dad and I are at the Swan tucking into a huge roast chicken dinner.

'Your mother and I used to come here when you and Nick were little.' Dad spears a carrot with his fork. 'Of course it was just a pub then, the only food you could get was a packet of cheese and onion and a pickled egg.'

Happy days. Nick and I would sit in the ancient Morris Marina with a packet of crisps and a bottle of pop while Mum and Dad had a drink in the pub. It was a big treat for us, although Social Services would probably be called in nowadays. Not that our parents did so bad; I grew up believing that only pubs served pop in small bottles – I had a real shock when I discovered you could buy them in shops.

I feel hugely relieved that Dad seems back to normal, he's perky and chatty, says he's even considering going to his gardening club this week. Brendan-the-neighbour hasn't been mentioned at all and I think maybe Jean is right and I'm fussing too much.

'Jean tells me you've been doing a bit of sorting out.'

'I have. That glory hole under the stairs was full of rubbish that'd been there for years and it needed doing. Jean offered to do it but I told her – I'm not that old and decrepit that I can't do a bit of spring cleaning. You have a look when we get back, you won't believe the difference.'

Dad insists on paying for lunch and I wrap up my left-over beef in a paper napkin to take home for Sprocket. The waitress is the same one who served Nick and I on Thursday night but she doesn't seem to remember me.

I'm not memorable like my brother. Or male.

'Wow, Dad that looks so much better – so nice and tidy.' We're back at Dad's for a post lunch cup of tea and he's proudly showing off his handiwork in the cupboard. It does look really neat and tidy and surprisingly large. Harry Potter could definitely live in this under stairs cupboard. The wallpaper of faded pink roses on a trellis brings back memories of my childhood, of waiting in the hall while mum wrestled Nick into his coat for school. The wrought iron coat hooks with coloured balls on the ends are long gone now as is the red stair carpet held down with brass stair rods that mum polished every week. I can remember the smell of that furniture polish even now. Strange how a piece of old wallpaper can trigger such vivid memories.

'See this,' says Dad, getting inside the cupboard and running his hand over the back wall. 'Have a look at this.'

I squeeze in next to him and look at his hand.

'What am I looking at Dad?' I can't see anything apart from a bit of ripped wallpaper.

'Here. Look. Behind this.' He carefully pulls the ripped piece of wallpaper down and points at the thumbnail sized piece of wall behind it.

I peer closer. 'What Dad? I can't see anything.'

'There. Look carefully.'

'Can't see a thing, Dad.'

He sighs, annoyed.

'THERE. LOOK. Behind the paper. The secret message.'

Secret message? I don't like the way this is going. I decide to humour him.

'Secret message? Who's it from?'

Dad looks at me as if I'm stupid and he can't believe what I'm asking.

He sighs. 'Well, MI5 of course.'

Chapter Four

'MI5? What messages are they leaving Dad? What do they say?'

'Look, there's another one there, and there.' He pulls more pieces of wallpaper down to show me the messages. There's nothing there except wall and when I ask him to tell me what they say he ignores the question.

'Look. Can't you see them?' He points to the wall and looks at me. Do I lie and humour him or say there's nothing there?

'I can't really see Dad, it's quite dark in here.'

This seems to satisfy him and he carefully smooths the wallpaper back against the wall.

'You mustn't tell anyone that I've shown them to you, I could get in trouble.' He chews on a gnarled finger. 'I'm an old fool I shouldn't have shown you. They won't be happy with me. Oh dear, oh dear me.' We come out of the cupboard and he starts pacing up and down the hallway.

'Shouldn't have done that,' he shakes his head as he paces up and down, 'I really shouldn't have done that.'

'No harm done, Dad. I couldn't read them anyway.'

'Shouldn't have told you. About MI5. It's secret, a secret mission.' He's walking faster and faster, talking faster and faster, repeating himself.

'I won't tell them, Dad, it'll be our secret.'

'They'll know. They'll KNOW.' He stops and almost shouts at me.

'Let's have that cup of tea, Dad,' I say in an effort to distract him. 'I don't know about you but I'm gasping.' I put my arms around him and hug him. To my surprise he doesn't push me away but lets me guide him out to the kitchen. He sits down on a stool at the breakfast bar. I fill the kettle with water and, as I plug it in to boil, I turn around and notice that the counter top is covered in keys. Large keys, small keys, tiny suitcase type keys, old rusty keys. All carefully laid out in neat rows. Where have they all come from? Dad has his head bent and is picking each one up and studying it carefully before putting it back down and picking up another. Hopefully he's forgotten about MI5.

'What are all the keys for Dad?'

'Looking for the key to the shed. I've searched everywhere in this house, cupboards, drawers, everywhere, and apart from the front and back door keys this is all of them. And I can tell you that none of them fit the shed. Someone has put a padlock on it and it wasn't me.' Dad crosses his arms defensively, 'SOMEONE is playing silly buggers in my garden.'

There's a challenge in the way he says it, as if he knows I'm not going to believe him.

'Okay Dad, why don't we drink our tea and then go and have a look?'

'All right. I suppose we could.'

As I get the milk out of the fridge and make the tea I can feel Dad's eyes on me but he doesn't speak. I pour the tea out and we sit and drink in silence. I can't quite believe how Dad can have changed so quickly; when we were eating our lunch he was completely normal, then suddenly he was talking about MI5. My mind is racing. Obviously, MI5 are not leaving messages in the cupboard under the stairs.

How can he be so normal one minute and then be seeing things that aren't there and imagining things the next? There's definitely something not right with him but what do I do? I need to take him to the doctors to get some advice but first I have to persuade him to go and I'm not sure how I'm going to do that. I pour another cup and we slurp our tea in an uncomfortable silence.

'Right,' says Dad, downing his mug, 'follow me.'

I've barely drunk any of my tea but I don't argue. God knows how he drinks it so hot. Dad unlocks the back door and goes out and I follow him down the garden, past the pink roses that are his pride and joy. I can smell them as we walk past and I'm transported back in time; Nick and I used to make rose petal perfume from the fallen petals and present the disgusting brown liquid to Mum in a milk bottle. She always pretended to be delighted and promised to wear it every day. I smile at the memory; Nick had thought making perfume was only for girls. In my bossy eight-year-old way I told him that chemists made perfume and they were always men; it was easy to persuade a six-year-old.

As we get further down the garden the neat borders give way to weeds and brambles, long and leggy grass that's gone to seed, trees that have grown unchecked. I turn and look back towards the house; it's completely hidden and it doesn't feel as though we're in a suburban garden anymore; we could be in the middle of the countryside. We reach the shed, the slats are grey and dried out, desperate for a coat of creosote. It's solid though, Dad made this shed himself and it was built to last. Eight foot by six with a pitched roof and a window running the whole length of one side.

'See. Look. New padlock and it's not mine.' He frowns, pointing at the padlock. He gives a good tug on it to make sure it's locked. It does look like a new padlock, a hefty one at that. But did Dad buy it and put it there himself and now he's forgotten? He could have, he forgot he rang me in a panic on Thursday so it's quite possible. And now I think of it how could Dad possibly see his neighbour down here? If we can't see the house from here then he couldn't possibly see the shed from the house.

'And that. I never put that there either.' He points at the window which is covered on the inside with what looks like sacking, blocking the view of anything inside. I press my nose up against the window and try to see inside but can't see a thing.

'It's him. That Brendan. He's put that lock on and those curtain things. Thinks I'm daft.'

So, he hasn't forgotten about his neighbour. Brendan just took a backseat while MI5 moved in.

The long grass around the shed is trodden down and flattened so I'm guessing Dad has been pottering around here quite a lot. He's doing it now, walking round and round, scrutinising it as he goes.

'Okay Dad,' I say, putting my hand under his elbow and steering him back towards the house before he starts to speed up and do the pacing thing again. 'Not to worry. We'll get Nick to have a look at it next time he comes down. He can crowbar the padlock off or something.' He allows me to almost push him towards the house and is silent as we trudge back up the garden. I can tell he's annoyed.

We go back into the house and Dad shuts the backdoor then carefully locks and bolts it and draws the curtain across. He then closes the window blinds.

'That'll stop him spying,' he says, 'and when I get *his* padlock off I'm going to put mine on there and that'll sort him out.' He then rechecks that the backdoor is locked and walks to the window to check the blinds are closed. He then goes back to the door and checks it again then the window, then the door. I need to stop him doing this pacing thing; he's going to wear himself out.

'Come on Dad, let's put the telly on. Antiques Roadshow will be on soon.'

He's bewildered as he stares at me and I can tell that he's trying to remember who I am. I put my arms around his shoulders and steer him through to the lounge and into his armchair. I put the TV on and Dad picks up the TV Times. We then have a completely normal conversation about what to watch and for the next hour Dad's his old self again. I begin to wonder if I've imagined it all, no more mention of secret messages or sheds at all.

When I leave I give him a kiss and get his usual 'drive carefully'. He seems quite content sitting in his armchair watching television. I let myself out of the front door and pause for a moment on the front step. I don't like leaving him, maybe I'll come and stay with him for a while. As I walk away I hear the sound of the deadlock being clicked down and the bolt pushed across.

Dad has locked himself in.

I slept really badly last night, tossed and turned and in the end, I gave up trying, turned the alarm off before it went off and got up. I must have been dreaming in the little bit of sleep I had as snapshots come back to me as I'm showering. I was in the shed making perfume out of padlocks and Nick was there and Mum too, but not Dad. Don't know what it all means but it suddenly hits me that I miss Mum and I wish she was here. We didn't have the easiest relationship, I always felt imprisoned by her rules and regulations, about having to be home much earlier than my friends if I went anywhere. I sometimes think I got married young so I could do what I liked. There were different rules for Nick, he had more freedom than me, maybe because he was a boy. I don't know, maybe if I had children of my own I'd understand more. But for all that I know I only had to ask and she would have done anything for me, given me anything. But I never did ask. Self-sufficient that's me, always have been.

I roughly towel dry my hair, rubbing briskly to get rid of my maudlin mood. Too late now. Get on with it.

Dressed and ready for work, Sprocket fed and harnessed up, I look at the clock and realise that I'm ready a whole hour early. I'll go to Linda's, she always up ridiculously early, she won't mind.

Anyway, I want to find out why she didn't tell me she knew Nick.

'You're early.'
'I know,' I say, following her through to the kitchen, 'bad night.'

'Coffee?'

'Please.'

'So what's up?'

I tell her a condensed version of the shed and MI5 episode.

'It's alright I don't mind if you laugh.' I can see the corners of her mouth twitching. It does sound comical, if it wasn't so bloody tragic it would be hilarious.

'I'm sorry. I know it's not funny at all, your poor dad. But MI5?'

I smile. 'I know, you couldn't make it up. I'm going to ring Nick later, see what we should do because I really don't have a clue.'

At the mention of Nick's name Linda turns around and busies herself wiping the already clean work top.

'So why did you never mention that you were at school with Nick? I've talked about him loads, you must have realised you knew him.' I say to her back. I'd meant to say it in a casual *it doesn't really matter way* but somehow it came out all wrong and sounds like I'm accusing her. Perhaps I am.

She pauses. 'I know. I feel a bit of an idiot but when I didn't tell you straight away I thought it'd look a bit odd if I suddenly said I knew him.'

'It does look odd. Especially as you met him last week and basically blanked him.'

Linda stops wiping the work top and turns around.

'Well there's no great secret. Glenda pretty much summed it up – I was a complete dork at school. To be honest I had a massive crush on Nick then and I just felt really embarrassed when I met him. I knew he'd never remember me. You didn't remember me either.'

'No, I didn't but be honest Linda, do you remember anyone from two years below you? I'll bet you didn't because anyone younger just wasn't on the radar.'

'No... you're right,' Linda concedes. 'It's just that school was absolute torture for me. I know it was getting on for thirty years ago but put the likes of Glenda in the same room as me and I'm thirteen years old again.'

'I know what you mean,' I say. 'It was the same for me. I wasn't one of the popular ones and I wasn't clever enough to be a swot so I was in no man's land too.'

Linda puts a bowl of dog food down on the floor while I hang onto Sprocket's lead to stop him hoovering up Henry's breakfast.

She stands up and pushes her hair back, 'Well, you weren't really, were you?' She raises an eyebrow at me.

'What do you mean?'

'Well, you were sort of cool. In an uncool way.'

'Cool? Me? I don't think so, anyway you didn't even know me!'

'No, I didn't, but I knew who you were, maybe because I fancied Nick. I used to see you around school and you always seemed so sure of yourself. You weren't part of a gang but I never saw anyone pick on you, or take the mickey. You always seemed to be your own person when the rest of us were trying to be like everyone else.'

I don't remember it like that at all. I was the same height at twelve as I am now. Five foot seven isn't very tall now but having a growth spurt a whole year before everyone else made me feel like a giant.

I shrug, 'Believe me Linda I wasn't cool at all. You

never saw me in a gang because no one would have me.'

'See. That's what I mean.' Linda smiles. 'You *were* cool but you didn't even know it.'

The clatter of Henry's empty food bowl spinning around the floor interrupts us and Linda bends down and picks it up. I unhook Sprocket's lead and he and Henry bound into the lounge. I look at the kitchen clock and realise that I'm going to be late if I don't get a move on.

'Shit, don't know where the time's gone, I'd better get off to work.' I pull a face. 'I'm really not in the mood for it today.' I'm not in the mood for anything. I feel adrift, as if I should be doing something but I don't quite know what.

'Okeydoke. Have fun.'

'Yeah, right.' I call over my shoulder as I let myself out of the front door.

Cool.

I don't think I've ever been called cool in my life.

But I like it, I definitely like it.

I park my car and just make it into the office before it starts raining. The mini heat wave is definitely over and it feels decidedly chilly. There's something different in the office and it takes me a good ten minutes to realise what it is. I can't smell cigarette smoke. Ralph is definitely in as the light is on in his office and the door's shut. I can smell something else though. Something sweet.

Rupert comes in just after me and Ian and Lucy make their customary last-minute appearance.

'Christ, it's vile out there,' says Ian, running his hand through his wet hair and shaking the rain off his

53

jacket. I look out of my window; the rain is coming down with a vengeance and I watch as a pigeon is caught on the wind and flung past at speed. Down in the precinct people are scurrying along clinging onto umbrellas as they battle against the rain. A gust of wind catches a plastic carrier bag and it swoops past the window like a wingless bird.

'Morning, Morning.' Ralph's office door is flung open with its usual force and Ralph appears. Normally he appears in a cloud of smoke but today there is nothing. In place of his normal cigarette he's holding an e-cigarette. So that was the sweet smell. He sucks deeply on it and exhales a stream of mist. A sweet strawberry smell drifts over.

'You've finally given up then Ralph?' says Rupert.

'Yep. Thought it was about time. A lot bleeding cheaper too. Been doing it since Saturday. Aim to get off this eventually but, slowly, slowly, catchy monkey.'

'I must say it has a very nice odour,' says Rupert, 'much nicer than cigarettes.'

'I've heard those things are worse than fags for you,' Ian chips in.

'Like I say, I intend to give it all up eventually. This'll just help to start with.'

'Yeah, that's what everyone says and they always end up back on the fags.' Ian is nervous when a fellow smoker attempts to give up. They're a dying breed, they don't want their smoking brothers to break ranks and join the other side.

'I've got some fags for when you get desperate Ralph.' Ian doesn't quite wave the packet under Ralph's nose but I know he wants to.

Ralph ignores him and sucks deeply on his e-cigarette and disappears back into his office. I boot up my computer and start the daily drudge. Surprisingly the next couple of hours fly by and I realise that I've actually been able to stop thinking about Dad for a while. At eleven o'clock I decide to make a coffee and ring Nick at the same time. I settle down in the tea room and close the door.

Nick answers on the third ring, 'Oh hello,' I say, caught out, 'you answered quickly, I thought I'd have to leave a message.'

'Na, Sis, day off today. Just got back from the gym. What's up?'

So I tell him.

'Christ, MI5? Where did that come from? What are we going to do? Is there a helpline or something we can ring?'

'I don't know. I think we need to get him to the doctors but I'm not sure how we're going to do it. Or what they can do when we get him there.'

'Tell you what,' says Nick, 'I haven't got any jobs for the next few days so I'll come down this afternoon and stay at Dad's for a few nights. I can keep an eye on him. We could concoct some story to get him to the doctors and take it from there.'

I feel a huge sense of relief; not just because Nick's going to stay at Dad's but because I've got a brother to share the worry with. How awful it would be if I had to do this on my own. We say our goodbyes and Nick promises to ring me when he gets to Dad's.

I take my coffee back to my desk feeling calmer, more in control. Everything's going to be okay. Nick and I will fix it.

An explosive bang disturbs the relative quiet of the office as Ralph's door flies open and bangs against the wall.

'Fuck's sake.' Ralph appears clutching his e-cig in his hand. 'Three days I've had it and the fucking thing won't work.' He's shaking it and clicking it and any minute I expect to see it launched across the office.

'Broken is it?' Smirks Ian.

'Forty quid I paid for this and look.' He clicks it several times. 'Dead, knackered.'

'Waste of money,' says Ian with authority. 'Everyone I know who's had one says they don't last five minutes.'

Ralph frowns and bangs the e-cig on the desk.

'Here, have one of these instead.' Ian offers Ralph his cigarette pack with a look of triumph. 'Have a proper smoke.'

'Ta,' says Ralph, reaching his hand out. As his pulls the cigarette from the packet he looks up at Ian's grinning face.

He hesitates. 'Na, you're alright,' he says, pushing the cigarette back into the packet and pulling his hand away. 'Think I'll pass.'

He turns and walks back into his office and closes the door. Quietly.

Everyone is speechless. The impossible has happened.

Ralph has given up smoking.

At quarter to five I get a text message from Nick:
Ring me ASAP
With a feeling of dread, I pick up the work's phone and dial his mobile.

He answers immediately.

'Nick? What's happened?'

'I'm at Dad's,' he's talking quietly. 'When I got here I couldn't get in the house, he'd put the deadlock down and he wouldn't open the door. Took me half an hour to persuade him. I don't think he knew who I was, Lou. I said, it's Nick, Dad, and he just kept saying well you would say that wouldn't you? You'll say anything to get in here. In the end I got him to look through the letterbox to make sure it was me but I don't think he was convinced.'

'What's he like now? Is he okay?'

'Depends what you mean by okay. All the curtains were shut and when he finally let me in he made me stand in the hallway, said that *they* would let him know when it was safe to let me in. Got to be honest Lou, he frightened me. Haven't seen him like that before.' Nick doesn't take anything seriously but I can tell he's shaken. 'After about ten minutes he let me in the lounge but we had to sit in the dark. Then he went out to the hall for a while then came back and said *they* said it was okay to open the curtains.'

I think I know why he went out to the hallway: he was checking for messages from MI5.

'Anyway, after a while he seemed a bit calmer so I said I'd come to stay for a few days for a bit of a break from London. He was fine with that and he seemed quite normal. He went to make a cup of tea and I took my bag upstairs to put in the back bedroom.' Nick paused. 'There were loads of cups of tea upstairs – in the spare room and Dad's bedroom. They were all full up, Lou. Anyway, I went downstairs and Dad's still in the kitchen, happy as Larry, making tea. So, I said to him what's with all the cups of tea upstairs then Dad? And do you know what he said?'

'No.' But I think I could hazard a guess.

'He says, they're for the agents. They've had me up and down those stairs all night making tea – I think they're taking advantage of me, I'm not getting any younger, you know. It's all very well those agents using my house as HQ but I'm an old man. They've been leaving the TV on all night as well. I woke up this morning and the TV had been on all night and they'd even put the gas fire on. He was so convincing when he said it, I almost went back upstairs and looked for them.'

I think we've been fooling ourselves hoping he would somehow magically get better. There's no point in false optimism, he's definitely getting worse.

'Do you think he's got a brain tumour or something? I just don't understand how he can have deteriorated so quickly. I'll ring the doctors now and get an emergency appointment for tomorrow. We'll just have to make up some story for him as to why he's got to go.'

'Okay.'

We're silent for a moment and I sense that there's something Nick's not telling me.

'And?' I prompt.

'Yeah, it gets worse.' Nick hesitates. 'He says he went round to the new neighbour earlier. Brendan.'

'Go on.'

'He says he feels quite aggressive towards him, says he told him to stay out of his garden and shed and that if he didn't he'd be sorry.'

'Oh Christ.'

'I know. And the cups of tea weren't the only thing I found in the bedrooms.'

'What else?' I ask with a sinking heart.

'Remember that old World War two German Luger?'

I remember it well. It was wrapped in a black cloth

58

inside a locked wooden box in the bottom of the sideboard. Occasionally Dad would get it out and show it to us but we weren't allowed to touch it. He bought it from an old junk shop when they still sold such things – he wasn't old enough to fight in the war – and I know he'd had it a long time. We were sworn to secrecy as he didn't have a licence for it and it should have been handed in, but it wasn't as if he'd ever even fired it.

'I remember.'

'It was on the dressing table. Cleaned. And loaded.'

Chapter Five

'I'm afraid we have no appointments left for today.'

It's only eight o'clock so how can all of the appointments be gone already? I'm tempted to not bother and put if off; pretend my Dad's not going mad and everything's alright.

But I can't. I feel like crying. I just want my old Dad back.

'Can I have an emergency appointment please?'

She sighs in a theatrical martyred way. 'That may be possible but you'll have to tell me what the symptoms are.'

I want to scream at her but I don't, I tell her my father is very confused and behaving strangely. There is silence for a few moments then she graciously says that if we take Dad at 9.30 he will be seen, adding that if he's late he will not be seen today. I fight the urge to ask her why she's working as a receptionist when she obviously hates speaking to people but decide this will probably result in no appointment ever, so keep my mouth shut. See, I do know when to shut up sometimes.

I bang the receiver down with a satisfying thump and flop down onto the settee. Sprocket jumps up onto me and rests his head on my chest and gazes into my eyes. I wrap my arms around him and nuzzle my face into his neck, breathing in his dogginess. He smells of warm biscuits and I stroke his ears as we snuggle in companionable silence.

I could stay like this all day, just sitting, not thinking. Perhaps if I sit here long enough Dad will return to normal and it will have all been a horrible dream. More of a nightmare. After a while I reluctantly get up and pick the phone up again.

Ralph answers on the second ring; I thought it'd be him as it's a bit early for everyone else. I lie and tell him that I have a migraine so won't be in to work today. I know that Ralph would have been fine if I'd told him the real reason but I just can't face talking about it.

'Ok girl, you get your head down and we'll see you tomorrow if you're feeling better. And don't worry about answering the phone, I'll put Ian on it.'

He's being so nice I feel even worse. I'm such a liar. And Ian won't be very happy to be tethered to his desk, either.

The weather's still miserable and wet so I put a jacket on before walking Sprocket round to Linda's. At the end of the street I see the familiar ears of The Truth approaching. I increase my pace so I don't get caught by him but as he gets nearer I'm shocked to see he has a black eye. He's looking at the pavement as he walks and would have walked straight past me if I hadn't called out to him.

'Morning, Norman!'

'Oh. Morningth.' He lisps through a fat lip. His face is scratched and grazed and he looks a mess. He makes no attempt to stop so I put my hand out and touch his arm.

'Are you okay?'

He stops and looks at me and draws a shaky breath, 'No, not reallyth. I got attacked.'

'Attacked?'

'Yeth. I was walking Lulu home on thunday night and she ran off, I remember hearing her barking and thath the lasth thing I remember. Woke up like thith.'

'Didn't you see anyone?'

'Don't think so. Can't remember. Hospital thay I'm concussed.'

'Where did it happen?'

'Back alley behind Roden Sthreet.'

That's only a couple of streets from here, why would someone attack Norman? He's well known in the area but I've never seen anyone show any malice to him.

'Surely you're not going to work?'

'No,' he says, swallowing hard, 'I'm looking for Lulu. She'th been missing sinth Thunday. I've looked everywhere.' His voice breaks, 'She'll be tho fwightened on her own, she doesn't like the dark. I don't know what I'll do if I don't find her.'

His eyes have filled up and he looks ready to cry. I pat him on the arm.

'I've looked everywhere. I think she's gone.' He sounds bereft.

'I'm sure she'll turn up Norman, she's probably just run off somewhere, she'll come back.'

'I'm starting to think she's been dog napped. She's a pedigree you know.' He sniffs.

I somehow doubt that dog nappers are going to be interested in an aging cream poodle.

'Listen Norman, I've got to go out now but when I take Sprocket out later I'll be sure to keep a look out for Lulu. I'm sure she'll turn up and be fine. Maybe someone's taken her in and is looking after her.'

'I hope tho.' He doesn't sound hopeful.

I watch as he trudges off despondently. Poor Norman, I know I'd be devastated if anything happened to Sprocket. I square my shoulders and march down the street dragging Sprocket behind me.

See? You're not the only one with problems Russell. Just get on with it.

We arrive at the doctor's surgery ten minutes early. Dad has been very quiet but compliant which is most unlike him. Nick has spun him some story about everyone over the age of 75 needing to have a blood test for diabetes. He said he might as well have not bothered with the lie because Dad didn't show any interest or questioned why Nick and I are taking him or why the doctor hasn't written to him. I wonder if he knows the real reason, if on some level he knows something is happening to him.

We sit either side of Dad on an uncomfortable red vinyl bench which faces reception. I'm sure there's one of these benches in every doctor's surgery that I've ever been in. Dad turns to look at me and I smile at him but he just looks at me blankly.

Strange how I had to almost to beg for an appointment but we're the only people in here.

'Christ, can't believe he still comes here. Thought the Krays would be dead by now. They must be nearly as old as dad,' Nick says looking around.

'Shssh.' I glance at Dad but he hasn't heard and looks deep in thought.

We used to come to this surgery when we were kids. The peeling posters on the walls might have changed but nothing much else has, the reception counter is the same but with many more coats of glossy cream paint and I'm sure the receptionist is the same one from my childhood. As if she senses me studying her she looks up from her paper shuffling, her tightly permed steel wool hairstyle glinting under the florescent tube light. She looks straight at me with pursed lips and a frown. I smile at her and she sniffs and goes back to shuffling paper.

At a quarter to ten Doctor McPherson pops his head around the door and calls Dad's name. The three of us troop in and stand in front of his desk like schoolchildren. We then have an awkward thirty seconds where we sort out the seating arrangements as there are only two uncomfortable looking metal chairs. I shove Dad into the one closest to the doctor and sit in the other chair. Nick hovers behind me.

'Now then Mr Russell, what can we do for you today?' Dr Ronald still has a Scottish burr even though he's lived here forever. His brother, Doctor Reginald Mcpherson is the other Victoria Street doctor, or Ronnie and Reggie Kray as Nick calls them. They're not twins but when we were kids we thought they looked the same, curly red hair and fuzzy beards. The red hair is white now.

Dad says nothing. Nick looks at me expectantly so I guess I'm doing the talking.

'Well, Dad has been getting very confused lately. He seems to think there are people in the house when there aren't and he's been seeing things as well. He's just not been himself at all.'

It sounds bizarre when I say it and I feel uncomfortable with the way Dr McPherson is looking at me. He taps away at his keyboard.

'He thinks there are MI5 agents staying in his

house and they're sending him secret messages through the cupboard under the stairs.' I'm speaking quietly so that dad can't hear what I'm saying. Doctor McPherson raises his eyebrows,

'He's been making cups of tea as well, for people who aren't there.' I don't tell him about the gun. 'And sometimes he doesn't know who we are.'

'Hmm. Mr Russell,' he says, turning to Dad. 'how are you feeling today?'

'I'm okay.' Says Dad. 'Don't know what I'm doing here though.'

'Just a bit of a check-up Mr Russell, shall we take your blood pressure, listen to your chest? Take some blood and a water sample. Water infections can make elderly people very confused you know.' He looks meaningfully at me.

We sit while Dad has his blood pressure taken, the only sound the puffing of the sphygmomanometer. Dr McPherson listens to Dad's chest with a serious look on his face. He puts the stethoscope away and taps a few more keys.

'If you can call into Nurse before you leave she can take some blood.' He places a plastic bottle on the desk, 'Take that home for a urine sample and pop it in when you're next passing. Now then Mr Russell, can you answer a few questions for me?'

Dad buttons his shirt up and looks at him and nods.

'Can you tell me who the prime minister is?'
'Theresa May.'
'Can you count backwards from 100 in 7s?'
Dad sighs. '100,93,86,79,72,65....'
'Good, good. Can you remember this name and address for me? John Scott, 23 Brown Road,

London.'

'Okay.' Dad looks at him suspiciously.

'Very good. Do you know what day it is today?'

'Of course I do, it's Tuesday.'

'Can you tell me what the time is?'

Dad looks at his watch. 'Ten to ten.' His mouth is set in a firm line now.

'Now, remember that name and address I asked you to remember? What was the name?'

'John Scott,' snaps Dad, 'and the address was 23 Brown Road, London. Why are you asking me all these stupid questions? I'm not daft you know.'

'No of course you're not but I understand from your daughter that you've been a bit confused lately, thinking someone's in your house when they're not, that sort of thing?'

Dad looks at me accusingly. 'Don't know what you're talking about Doctor. There's no one living in my house except me. Maybe *she's* the one that's confused.'

It's very quiet in the car on the way home. Dad is deep in thought and hasn't spoken to me or Nick since we came out of the surgery. He'd sat and had his blood taken without comment and tucked the sample bottle in the top pocket of his jacket without saying a word. I almost doubt myself, perhaps I'm the one that's going round the bend. It's been a waste of time – what did I expect? A magic pill that would make everything normal again? I feel mean and horrible and I just want to get home.

I sit in the back of the car gazing out of the window. I remember this route through the Raleigh Estate so well from my childhood. Frogham's oldest council estate, it wasn't too bad then but has got progressively worse. If you were brought up on the Raleigh you tend to keep it quiet. It's large and well-spaced and the houses are built of some sort of grey concrete, not attractive, but good family houses. We pass one house which has been painted a vivid pink, the paint peeling off. The majority of the houses have unkempt gardens with assorted unwanted mattresses and settees, peeling paintwork and overfilled dustbins. We pass an exception, the garden neatly tended with pretty flower beds and bright white net curtains.

It's depressing. We pass a children's play park and I watch as three tracksuit-bottomed boys throw stones at a bedraggled dog which is cowering under a tree.

'Stop the car!'

'What?'

'STOP THE CAR! NOW!'

'Okay, okay.' Nick pulls into the side of the road. 'Where's the fire, what are we stopping for?'

I jump out of the car and start running towards the boys. I can hear Nick calling me but I keep running.

'LEAVE THAT DOG ALONE!' I shout as I get nearer to the stone throwers.

They turn and look at me with grubby faces that are far too cynical for their ten years. The biggest of the three pauses with his hand in the air mid throw.

'Fuck off,' he says in a bored voice. The other two snigger.

'OI! Clear off and torment someone else.' Nick has followed me and is striding towards us. They look at him then back to me again.

'You deaf or something? Clear off!' Nick booms at them.

'Oh yeah? Gonna make us mister?'

'If you like.' Nick marches towards them.

'NICK! Leave them!'

He ignores me and carries on walking.

'Leave me alone you paedo! I'll tell the police on ya,' the older boy squawks.

Nick towers over him. 'Oh yeah?' He pulls his phone out of his pocket. 'I'll call them, shall I? Don't suppose you'll be a stranger to them.'

'We were going anyway, this is boring.' The boy shrugs, an uncertain look on his face. He half-heartedly throws the stone in his hand at the dog then saunters off dragging his feet. The two smaller boys follow him, turning occasionally to show us they're leaving because they want to, not because Nick's told them to.

'Christ what a dump.' Nick scans the street. 'Don't remember it being this bad when we were kids. I wouldn't want to come here after dark. And what are you playing at Lou? I thought there was some sort of emergency, not a bloody dog.' He looks peeved and I can see Dad watching us from the car.

'It's not a bloody dog,' I say sulkily, marching towards the dog. 'It's Lulu, and we're taking her home.'

Lulu is rooted to the spot; I'd been afraid she might run off before I got to her. I put my hand on her back and gently stroke her, she doesn't move and I can feel her shaking.

'It's okay, Lulu, it's okay,' I say soothingly. 'We'll soon have you home.'

I wrap my arms around her and pick her up and hold her tight. She barely weighs anything and is cold, damp and shivering.

'You want to bring THAT in my car?'

'Well I'm not going to leave her here.'

'So you're into rescuing stray dogs now, are you?'

'She's not a stray – she's my friend's dog and she's been lost for days.' Norman would be thrilled to hear me call him my friend.

''For Christ's sake. Okay. But I'm warning you if it makes a mess you're paying for a full valet.'

'Nick?'

'What?'

'Stop being a knob.'

He frowns and then laughs, 'Okay. C'mon, let's go before someone nicks my wheels.'

'Do you think the doctors visit was a waste of time?' I ask Nick as we pick our way back to the car over discarded McDonalds wrappers and broken bottles.

'I don't know.' We stop for a moment. 'He seemed perfectly normal in there, passed all the tests. Maybe he's better now. Maybe we're making too much of it.' He sighs. 'I don't know Lou, I just don't know.'

'I feel the same,' I say. 'I felt like a fraud in there – as if we were making it up or exaggerating or something. But then I think back over the last few months and I know there's something wrong with him, he's not right.'

'There *is* something wrong but to an outsider he can appear completely normal – I mean, Jean hasn't mentioned any concerns about him has she and she sees him a lot.'

'No, she hasn't,' I say, 'but she's not really the observant sort, yeah, she sees him a lot but she's mostly tidying and making him a sandwich and talking *at* him, so she probably wouldn't notice.'

'What happens now? I can stay for a few more days but then I'll have to go back to London.'

'We have to wait for the test results. Maybe it's a water infection that's sent him doolally.'

'I honestly don't know what we'll do if the tests come back okay. Ask the doctor for help I suppose?' Nick looks rueful. 'God knows.'

We arrive back at the car; Dad stares at me impassively through the window, I smile at him but he blanks me. I get into the back and settle with Lulu on my lap. She's not shaking quite so much and takes a tentative lick of my hand. She has dried blood on her leg and ear; I run my fingers over her leg and she flinches a bit, Norman will have to get her checked over.

'Christ, that dog stinks.' Nick starts the engine.

'So would you if you'd been out in the rain for two nights.'

Dad doesn't turn around or talk to me, or ask why we have a dog in the car. He doesn't talk to Nick either so we're both getting the blame for the visit to the doctors.

'Drop me off at mine Nick. I'll come round Dad's later.'

I need to reunite Lulu with Norman and put him out of his misery. I need to get changed too, Nick's right; Lulu stinks.

'I don't know how I can ever thank you enough, I can't believeth you found her.'

An overjoyed Lulu is licking Norman's face and he has the biggest smile ever.

'I just don't understand how she got all the way over to the Raleigh – it's miles away.'

I can't understand it either. She was frozen to the spot when I found her. I can't imagine her running for miles, she'd be more likely to hide.

'Who's that Norman? Who's at the door?' A woman's querulous voice calls from a doorway. I can hear the drone of studio applause and see the flickering blue light of a television through the net curtains.

'ITH LULU. MOTHER, LULU'THHOME.'

'She'th a little bit deaf,' he says to me. 'Come in and meet Mother, she'll want to thank you as well.' Norman opens the door wider.

I stay on the door step. 'I can't stop Norman I have to get back to work, maybe another time.' I back down the path to the gate.

'Thank you tho much. I thought I'd never thee Lulu again. You saved her life.'

I smile and wave. 'My pleasure.'

'You saved her life, you did. And that's the God'th honest truth.'

Yep. He'll be fine.

'I think you should go.'

'Be better if you went, woman's touch and all that.'

I give Nick an old-fashioned look.

'What?'

'Why does it have to be me?' I hiss. 'I had to do the talking this morning at the doctors and now Dad won't even talk to me let alone look at me.' It's true. He's totally ignored me, it's as if I'm not here. I know it's bad when I haven't even been offered a cup of tea. The lounge door is shut and we're standing in the hallway trying to talk quietly. Jean is in the lounge dusting and I can hear the twittery sound of her voice as she talks to Dad. I know she's wondering what's going on and we're going to have to tell her soon.

'Well then it makes sense,' says Nick. 'You're already in the dog house so it won't make any difference if you go 'cos you know he's not going to like it when he sees you go round there.'

'We can wait and go when he's not looking. He doesn't need to know.'

'He'll know,' says Nick. 'He never misses anything, somehow, he'll know. Even if he is doolally.'

It's true, he will. I'm sure he has a sixth sense. One of us has to go next door and apologise to the neighbour for Dad's threatening visit and it looks like it's going to be me.

'We could just not bother,' Nick goes on. 'It's not like we know him or ever see him.'

'We can't do that – what if dad does it again? We need to make him aware of the situation. Just in case.'

'Just in case of what?'

'I don't know. Just in case. Anyway, I don't want him thinking badly of Dad.'

Nick doesn't say anything. I give in.

'Okay I'll go. Try and keep Dad away from the window, I'd rather he didn't know.'

I wait until Dad goes into the kitchen to make yet another cup of tea, although I'm not offered one, and slip quietly out of the front door and down the driveway. I walk quickly past the hedge and into next door's garden. A long, neat, printed concrete driveway – which I'm not keen on – with room for at least four cars, curves towards the house. Double fronted bay windows. A very big house for one person, but then so is Dad's.

I just hope he's in because I don't want to have to

go through this again. There's a people carrier parked in front of the house that I'm guessing is what he uses for his airport runs. Hopefully he's in.

I can't find a bell so rattle the letter flap, then rattle it a bit more in case he doesn't hear it. The door is opened almost immediately and I wonder if he's watched me walk up the drive. I don't know what I was expecting but it's not what opens the door. He's huge, not huge fat but huge tall. At least six foot four with hands the size of coal shovels and a massive chest with a red T-shirt the size of a tablecloth stretched across it. God knows how he fits inside the taxi. I can see why Dad feels intimidated by him.

'Hello.' His voice is a shock; he's softly spoken. Not the voice you'd expect from someone so big.

'Hello. Sorry to bother you. I'm Louise, Tom's daughter. From next door.'

'Hello.' He puts his hand out, 'Brendan. Pleased to meet you.' I shake his hand expecting him to pulverise my fingers but his handshake is surprisingly gentle.

'I've come to apologise. For yesterday. On behalf of Tom. My Dad.'

'Oh.' He looks surprised.

'Yes. I'm sorry if he was rude to you and maybe a bit, ah, aggressive. He's not very well at the moment.' I feel disloyal and traitorous talking about Dad. 'He doesn't mean it. I mean, he can't help it. He's not usually like it. He's really very nice. And polite. The nicest man you could ever meet. Normally.' I'm blathering.

'Honestly, he wasn't rude at all. There's no need to apologise. He's always been the perfect gentleman to me. I'm sorry to hear he's not well.'

'Oh.' I'm surprised. 'He told us he's been round and well, he told us what he said and it wasn't very nice.'

'He did come round but, um, anyway, I'm glad you've called round, I often see your car there and was hoping to catch you.' So he was watching through the window. 'Without your Dad knowing,' he adds. I wonder what he's going to say.

'Yesterday wasn't the first time Tom came round. He's been round five times in the last few weeks. I'm concerned for him, which is why I've been hoping to catch you.'

'Oh.' I don't know what to say.

'He asks the same question every time.' He clears his throat looking uncomfortable.

'What does he ask?' But I don't want to know really.

'He asks me if I've seen his wife. Says he's looked everywhere but he can't find her.'

And then I do the stupidest thing.

I start to cry.

Chapter Six

Nick went back to London a week ago and Dad seems to have settled down; no more strange behaviour, no more M15 or intruders in the garden. But I feel unsettled, a calm before the storm feeling. Almost as if I'm waiting for something to happen.

Dad seems to have forgiven me and is speaking to me again although the visit to the doctors hasn't been mentioned. He's not the same though, it's as if he's playing a part, carefully acting how he used to be. There's an awkwardness between us that never used to be there; the conversation is stilted, and it never used to be. I've taken Sprocket on my last couple of visits as a distraction and Dad didn't seem to mind - which is unusual in itself. I've kept Nick informed and we speak most days, but I wish he was here. It's much easier when there are two of us.

The test results all came back fine and I think I always knew that they would. No underlying illness, no water infection. I made another appointment to see Dr McPherson but I didn't take Dad, I went on my own as I'm sure Dad wouldn't have come even if I'd asked him.

Dr McPherson was reluctant to do anything and suggested we wait and just monitor Dad's behaviour. He really frustrated me, and I got the feeling that he thought I was exaggerating. If it wasn't for the fact that Nick has witnessed Dad's strange behaviour, I'd doubt myself. In desperation I told him about the gun and that I feared what might happen. He then begrudgingly said that he'd refer Dad to the mental health team. They rang me the next day with an appointment for three weeks' time to assess him. I asked if they could see him sooner but apparently, he's not a priority as he isn't *in crisis*. Whatever that means. I feel sorry for people who don't have anyone to fight for them; if Dad was on his own he could quietly go mad. Or shoot someone. I'm not sure how I'm going to persuade Dad to go for the appointment, but I'll worry about that when it happens.

I haven't told Dad that the results have come back okay, mostly because I've lied to him and told him that Dr McPherson says he can't drive until he gets the all clear. I don't want him getting in his car if he's seeing things, what if he had an accident or knocked someone over?

Nick and I told Jean about Dad, she was shocked and disbelieving but said she would keep an eye on him. She said several times that she's never noticed any odd behaviour from Dad and what a shock it was, how surprised she was. I didn't like the way she looked at Nick and I. Almost accusing.

Brendan, the next-door neighbour, was really kind when I started blubbing on his doorstep. He asked me in for a cup of tea but I refused so he went off and came back with a giant piece of kitchen paper, so I could blow my nose. I don't think he knew quite what to do with himself. He patted me awkwardly on the shoulder with a massive paw like hand and said 'there, there.' I'd have laughed if I hadn't been feeling so miserable. I'd composed myself before I went back to Dad's but Nick noticed straight away.

'What's the matter? Did he have a go at you, I'll go and sort him out...'

'No. No, he didn't have a go at me at all, he was really nice. It's just me. Being stupid.'

'Come here.' Nick wrapped me in a bear hug. 'It'll be alright Lou, it'll get sorted.'

I let myself be hugged. 'It won't be alright though, will it? It's just going to get worse and I can't bear it.' I told Nick what Brendan had said about Dad looking for Mum and that started me blubbing again.

'Okay,' Nick said, 'one thing at a time. We just have to take it one step at a time. That's all we can do. There must be some treatment for whatever's wrong with Dad. There's a pill for everything nowadays.'

'What if it's a brain tumour? What if there's no treatment? I can't bear it Nick, I just can't bear it.'

'C'mon now, let's not jump ahead, we've just got to deal with what's happening now. We'll drive ourselves mad if we try and diagnose him ourselves. Let's just wait and see.' I think he's saying this to convince himself as much as me.

'Okay. One step at a time.'

'I'm here for a couple more days so I'll go next door and speak to Simon and Eileen, get them to keep an eye on him. In case he goes knocking on doors again. They've lived there for years and Dad always speaks quite fondly of Simon so I'm sure they won't mind. I'll give them my mobile, so they can hold of me if they need to.'

I have a sudden panicked thought, 'What about the gun? What have you done with the gun?'

'Don't worry it's sorted. I've left the gun where Dad put it, but I've taken the bullets out.'

'What, you threw them out?'

'No. Didn't know what to do with them – I didn't think I could just chuck them in the bin.'

'So where are they?'

'I put them in Mum's sewing box, he'll never look in there.'

He won't. The sewing box has been in the back bedroom since Mum died and Dad would never think to look in there.

'How did you get the bullets out? We only ever watched Dad do it. I wouldn't have a clue how to do it.'

'Easy. I used to get it out and play with it all the time when we were kids. I knew where Dad kept the key and I used to practise loading it and reloading it.'

'You sly sod.' I'm shocked.

Nick laughs. 'Used to pretend I was Clint Eastwood.' He narrows his eyes, pointing his finger at me. 'Go ahead, punk, make my day.'

'There's another woman missing.' Rupert announces to the office putting down the receiver. 'They haven't given any details yet, but we should get a name later on today.'

Even though Rupert hasn't spoken loudly Ralph has come out of his office. Strangely, his hearing seems to have improved since he stopped smoking. He's dispensed with the e-cigarette and moved onto boiled sweets now. He won't have any teeth left if he carries on munching away on them at the current rate. He looks better though, not so grey.

'Is that all you've got?' he asks Rupert.

'Yes. Details to follow later. Apparently, a woman was reported missing on Monday morning and they haven't been able to locate her, so she's now listed as missing.'

Ralph crunches on a humbug, 'Do they think she's linked to the other missing one? She still hasn't turned up.'

'Well, obviously they're not saying, but that's the assumption everyone will jump to.'

This is big news for the Frogham Herald; we've run the missing woman story a couple of times a week since the Crimewatch appeal, but it's basically been a rehash of the first article as there haven't been any sightings of her. The recording equipment on my telephone has never been used as the *Scottish lady* has never rung back. We've all pretty much written her off as a crank.

'Maybe we've got a serial killer in Frogham,' says Ralph. 'Imagine the papers we could sell. I can see the headlines now – *the Frogham Ripper strikes again* or *Killer strikes fear in the heart of Frogham.*'

'Steady on Ralph. We're still hoping Suzanne Jenkins will be found safe and well,' Rupert says disapprovingly. Unusually for a reporter Rupert has moral standards. Probably why he's working for the Frogham Herald and not Fleet Street anymore.

'Na, don't mean to wish her ill or anything.' Ralph looks slightly uncomfortable. 'I just meant it would make good copy – you know what I mean Rupert, being a journalist and all. Doesn't mean I want anything bad to happen.'

'Hey, look at this,' calls Ian who's hanging out of the open window. 'Looks like we're really in the news.'

We all crowd around the window and look down into the precinct. A white van with a *West Today* logo on the side is attempting to park on the pavement in front of Superdrug.

'Bloody cheek!' says Ralph. 'That's not even a road, they shouldn't be parking there.' He sniffs the air and turns to Ian and says in an accusing tone, 'You been smoking out of the window?'

He has; I can see ash all over the floor.

'No, of course not.' Ian is indignant, blushing scarlet. 'I knew this would happen when you gave up, you're turning into one of those sanctimonious ex-smokers.'

'No, I'm not,' says Ralph. 'But there is a smoking ban you know. You can't smoke indoors – you should know that. You want to give it up. Filthy habit.'

Ian looks at him with disbelief. 'Never stopped you though did it? You needed a knife to cut through the smoke in your office.'

'I've seen the light my boy. Seen the light.' Ralph sniffs. 'It is actually an offence you know. If I reported you, you could get an eighty quid fine.'

Ian opens his mouth to reply and Lucy buts in. 'Look. They're getting out.' Lucy points her finger at the van in an attempt to distract them. 'I'm sure I've seen her on the news.'

We watch as a man and a woman get out of the vehicle. The man walks to the back of the van and inspects the large satellite dish attached to the back.

'They must think there's a story – how did they find out so quickly?' asks Lucy.

'Same way I did – the police report. No doubt the precinct will be full of TV vans by tonight.' Rupert tuts.

The woman is now standing in front of the bakers and the man is holding a pole with a furry microphone hanging in front of her.

As if on cue another van turns into the precinct and attempts to park in front of Fine Foods. The suited figure of the manager appears from the supermarket and strides over to the van and what looks like a heated discussion between the manager and driver follows.

After a lot of arm waving and pointing the van slowly moves away from the supermarket and down to where the precinct meets the road. The van then parks half on and half off the pavement whilst the supermarket manager stands watching from the pavement, arms folded.

'I hope we get a name soon,' Ralph says. 'We need to get it in tonight's paper. Bloody TV. Don't want them beating us to it.'

'But they will, won't they?' says Ian. 'They always do.'

'Not the same as reading my boy, not the same. People like to digest the facts, that's why newspapers will never die.'

'Hope you're right Ralph otherwise we'll all be out of a job.'

We drift back to our desks and it sets me thinking. The missing woman is just a news story to all but those closest to her; a real-life soap opera with the media eagerly awaiting the next instalment. I click on the news link and ponder Suzanne Jenkins' photograph. She has one of those familiar faces, or maybe I've just studied this picture too much.

At lunchtime I pop down to Fine Foods to buy my lunch. The TV vans have now grown to three; West Today, BBC West and Wales Central. You'd think they could just send one and share it.

A blonde with thick orange foundation is practising her piece to camera, standing in front of the Fine Foods doorway despite the manager shooing the van away earlier. I'm a bit disappointed to see her reading the script from her phone. I thought it'd be a bit more glamorous than that, more lights, camera, action! I squeeze by her saying 'excuse me' so I can get inside to buy my cheese and pickle sandwich and she tuts loudly and gives me a filthy look.

As I'm paying for my sandwich at the self-service till a bearded man in a bobble hat starts shouting at the till.

'SHUT UP. Just SHUT UP.' He yells it every time it tells him to insert his credit card. When he starts to kick the machine the security guard ambles over from his usual perch by the door and, with a bored look on his face, propels him to the exit. He goes quietly, and I have the feeling that it's a regular occurrence. An assistant appears and removes his unpaid for bottle of cider from the basket and takes it away. They should really have had the cameras inside, there's more going on.

When I get back to the office Ralph is still prowling around like a caged animal. He's been like this since Rupert got the news of the missing woman this morning. He keeps looking over at Rupert as if he can will the name to come through.

'I've got a name!' shouts Rupert suddenly, 'And they're sending over a photo now to go in tonight's paper.'

'About bloody time,' yells Ralph.

'Her name is Glenda Harris, age 42, lives in Vilett Gate.'

What? Who? Glenda? Surely not. There are lots of people called Glenda. Aren't there?

'That's not her that owns the salons is it? Sure I know the name, was at some business do I went to.' Ralph wanders over to read over Rupert's shoulder.

'Not sure. They're releasing more information with the photo.'

'Isn't Vilett Gate near where the other one lived? Lives,' says Lucy.

'Don't know. Let's Google it.' Rupert opens Streetview. 'It is. The next street more or less, although the first one lives in a flat and these are posh houses. Very close though.'

'They could know each other. Lev lives around there doesn't he?' Ian chips in.

'Yeah, he does.'

Ian smirks.

'So what are you implying Ian?' Ralph raises his eyebrows in question; he looks annoyed.

Lucy and I exchange raised eyebrow glances too.

'Nothing,' says Ian, 'Just making an observation.'

'Lots of people live there, houses full of people.'

'I know. Just saying.'

Rupert interrupts. 'They've just sent the photo over.'

We all gather round Rupert's PC.

I recognise the glossy hair, the slightly petulant expression.

It is her. It's Glenda, Linda's old school friend.

'Have you heard?' I ask Linda as I struggle with an excited Sprocket and fight to get his harness on him while he tries to lick my face.

'Heard what?' I can tell she hasn't.

'About Glenda.'

'What about Glenda?' She looks at me with her eyebrows raised. 'Don't tell me she tried to befriend you on Facebook. Take my advice and ignore her.' She laughs.

'Um, no.'

'What?'

'She's gone missing, has been missing since Monday. The police are putting out an appeal to see if anyone's seen her.'

'Shit. No, I didn't know, had no idea but then I haven't seen the news. What do you mean by missing?'

'Apparently, she's been reported as missing since Monday, she didn't turn up for a business meeting and no-one has seen her. Might be nothing but everyone is linking her to the other missing woman.'

'God. I don't like her but wouldn't wish anything bad on her. We only saw her what . . . less than a couple of weeks ago.'

'I know, it's unbelievable. Doesn't seem real.'

'I thought she'd been quiet on Facebook. She'd messaged me loads and then she didn't bother after the barbeque. Thought I'd offended her, and she wasn't going to bother with me anymore. Felt relieved to be honest. Feel really bad now.'

'You should tell the police about Facebook – might help them pinpoint exactly when she went missing.'

'I will.' Linda's on her phone Googling the appeal number already. 'Poor Glenda, I hope they find her and it's all been a misunderstanding.'

'Me too. But not likely – the fact that she never turned up for the meeting was most unlike her.

Someone went round to her house and ended up calling the police when they couldn't contact her.'

'I know she was living with someone for a few years but that broke up about six months ago I think. Which was probably why she contacted me. Wanted to hook up with old friends. Maybe she's gone off on holiday and not told anyone.'

'Maybe.'

But neither of us really thinks so.

Dad opens the front door and Sprocket and I follow him through to the lounge. There's something different in this room but I can't quite place what it is. The furniture's the same, the oodles of ornaments are the same, but something's askew. I can smell lavender furniture polish and I remember that Jean's been in today. Friday is housework day.

Dad is engrossed in the news which gives me an opportunity to study him. He looks quite pale and tired and I think he's lost weight. I wish I could do something to make everything alright again. I ask him if he's seen the report about the missing woman. I wonder whether to tell him I knew her. Know her.

'Yes,' he says, 'saw it on the afternoon news. What's the world coming to eh? They haven't found the other one yet either. It's not looking good.' I'm grateful that he sounds quite coherent.

I agree with him and we chat about it and I tell him about the television crews in the precinct. I even get a laugh out of him when I tell him about Ralph giving up smoking. He really does seem like his old self tonight and the conversation flows easily.

And then it hits me, the something that's different. The wall above the fireplace has always been full of family photographs: Mum and Dad's wedding and anniversary photos, Nick and I as babies, toddlers, teenagers, adults. You could document our family's lives from those photos.

The pictures are all still there but in different places; they've all been moved. I can see the wallpaper is slightly faded in places where they've been moved around.

I open my mouth to ask Dad why he's moved them, then stop myself. He can move them around if he likes, he doesn't have to explain himself to me.

Sprocket scratches at the lounge door so I clip his lead back on and take him through to the kitchen.

'Won't be long Dad.' I don't think Dad has even heard me as he's engrossed in the television. We go out of the back door and I wander around the garden with Sprocket while he finds a suitable spot. When he's finished I carry on down the garden towards the shed.

The shed looks just the same as the last time I looked at it and the padlock looks the same as well. Dad hasn't changed it. Sprocket starts to whine as we get closer and I pull at his lead but can't get him to go any closer than about two feet away. He's such a wimp sometimes, maybe there's a mouse in there, or even a rat.

'See – even that dog of yours knows there's something wrong with that shed.' Dad has followed me outside and I jump as he speaks.

'Blimey Dad you frightened the life out of me.' I laugh.

'I want Nick to cut that padlock off. It's not mine you know. It's his.' He nods in the direction of Brendan's house. 'Next door.'

'You could do with some more plants in those pots Dad, a bit of colour,' I say to distract him. I wander over to three large tubs that have dying bedding plants in them. 'Something for the summer.' I'm surprised when Dad follows me and lets the subject of the shed drop.

'Hmm.' he pulls a few leaves off the plants. 'They do look a bit sorry for themselves. These were your mother's pride and joy. She was the one that did the planting, had green fingers she did.' It's the first time he's mentioned Mum in weeks. In the dark days after she died he couldn't even say her name without choking up, none of us could. Gradually he started talking about her again and thinking back he would often mention her, 'your mother this' or 'your mother would have liked this.' She was still a big part of his life. He always expected to go before her; I don't know why he thought that, but he did. He used to say that he knew Nick and I would look after her when he'd gone and that was a comfort to him. A massive heart attack that none of us were expecting and Mum was gone. Not even a chance to say goodbye.

He's studying the leaves, lost in thought. When Mum died we were all reeling with shock; the three of us were grieving yet Dad seemed so strong and capable like he always was that Nick and I leaned on him. He supported us, and we should have supported *him*. Poor Dad. Mum was his whole life, his soul mate, we should have helped him more. I don't know what I could have done but looking back now I can see that I didn't do enough, I didn't understand his devastation.

'I could take you to the garden centre tomorrow – get some more plants then go and have a bit of lunch at the Swan, what do you think?'

Dad visibly brightens, 'That's not a bad idea, be a change of scenery from being stuck here.' I know this is a bit of dig at me because he can't drive himself. But he says it with a smile, so I think I'm forgiven.

'I'll pick you up about ten?'

'Yes.' Dad looks almost cheerful, 'I'll look forward to that.'

We trundle back indoors, and I feel a glimmer of hope; if he can be so normal most of the time perhaps he'll be okay. Maybe he's just been going through a bad patch.

Dad fills the kettle and puts it on to boil, he walks over to Sprocket who's lying on the doormat.

'Does he want a biscuit? Will he eat a custard cream?'

'I'm sure he will, Dad, he'll eat anything.'

Dad gets the biscuit tin out of the cupboard and looks at Sprocket who immediately guesses that food is on offer. In seconds he's sitting in front of Dad expectantly.

Dad holds out a custard cream and I pray that Sprocket doesn't bite his hand off and spoil the moment. Sprocket takes it from him daintily and swallows it whole.

'Good boy.' Dad pats Sprocket on the head. 'There's a good boy.'

I really think everything's going to be alright.

Chapter Seven

The alarm goes off and I wake to the sound of the eight o'clock news. I lie in bed and watch the sunlight filtering through the curtains, the dappled pattern giving the room an underwater look. I enjoy the feeling of peace, the weight of a snoring Sprocket across my feet. It's the first time in weeks I've slept all night without waking; the first time I haven't woken before the alarm's gone off.

I'm feeling optimistic after my visit to Dad yesterday; he seemed so like his old self. I'm looking forward to today and once we've had lunch I'm going to help him plant his pots up with new plants.

The newsreader is repeating the news of Glenda's disappearance and for a moment I feel guilty for feeling happy when who knows what's happened to her.

I shower and dress and take Sprocket for a quick walk around the block before I leave for Dads. It's going to be a lovely day, the sun is out, and the air is warm, summer's arrived, again. I lift my face to the sun as I walk along enjoying the warmth.

We get back and I change out of my trainers and go and fetch my handbag. Sprocket's no fool, he knows that I'm going out, so he lies under the kitchen table, right at the back.

'Come on, you big baby,' I say, dragging him out

from under the table by the scruff of his neck. 'I'll come back and get you after we've been to the garden centre and you can come to the Swan. We can sit in the garden.' He's having none of it and looks at me accusingly, leaving the proffered treat on the floor.

Honestly, talk about spoilt, worse than a kid.

I arrive at Dad's at bang on ten o'clock. I expect he'll be waiting in the hallway with his jacket on ready to go.

I'm surprised to find the front door is ajar; I go in but Dad's not waiting in the hallway he's at the top of the stairs. He doesn't have his jacket on, but he does have the chest of drawers from his bedroom balanced precariously at the top of the stairs.

'DAD,' I shout, 'What are you doing?'

'Oh hello,' he says with a big smile on his face. 'Just getting rid of this to make way for the equipment.'

'WHAT?'

'Stand back. It's coming down.' He gets behind the chest of drawers ready to push. I bound up the stairs two at a time and somehow manage to stop the chest of drawers from crashing down the stairs. Dad looks bewildered and I shout at him.

'WHAT ARE YOU DOING?'

'I have to get rid of...

I cut him off. 'It's going back in the bedroom. NOW.' With strength I didn't know I had I push it back towards the bedroom, it's old and heavy, probably built to withstand bombing.

'Help me Dad, help me push it back,' I bark at him. Dad meekly does as I say, and I feel horrible for shouting at him. We get it through the doorway into his bedroom and I stop to catch my breath. I look around in disbelief, unable to process what I'm seeing. The bed has been stripped, the stripes of the bare mattress on show. The room is a shell with just furniture and nothing else, no bedding, no ornaments, gone are the books that are usually piled on the bedside cabinet, the curtains have been taken down from the window. How can I have not noticed that when I got out of the car? Because I wasn't looking that's why. I was in my own little happy bubble which has now well and truly exploded. I want to cry.

'Where is everything Dad? What have you done with it all?'

'Oh, it's out in the back garden.' He says brightly. 'Going to burn it all later, have no need for it now. They're moving the intelligence equipment in soon, so I need to get all this stuff out. Get rid of it all.' He looks really pleased with himself.

Dear God, what am I going to do? I wish Nick was here.

'Well,' I need to humour him and distract him, 'how about we have a cup of tea and a breather before we get on with it?' He looks doubtful. 'I'm sure you're allowed a tea break,' I add.

'Okay. But we'd better not stop for too long though.'

I practically push Dad through the doorway and down the stairs. We go through to the kitchen and Dad settles himself at the table.

'So,' I say as I fill the kettle, 'did you realise that you'd left your front door open Dad? It was open when I got here.' I put the kettle on to boil.

'Was it?' he looks confused. 'I haven't been out the front today. I took everything out of the back door.' I look through the kitchen window; clothes, books, ornaments and lamps are heaped in a massive pile on the patio.

'Do you think you might have left it open all night?' I ask with a sinking feeling.

'Ah yes, of course. I forgot. I went out last night to check on the street. There was definitely something going on and I walked down to the end of the street for a recce. Didn't see anything but I think they were hiding. They know I'm onto them you see.'

So, the door's been open all night. I wonder how many times that's happened. I pour Dad a cup of tea and put it on the table for him. I'm at a loss, I really don't know what to do.

Then I see it, looking through the doorway into the hallway I can see the telephone table and seat. The telephone is an old-fashioned cream one with big buttons, it's been there for years. It's now in pieces; every part has been carefully unscrewed and prized apart and if it wasn't for the number buttons it wouldn't even look like a telephone. I put my cup down and walk into the hallway for a closer look. It's been unplugged from the wall; the telephone socket has been unscrewed and there's a pile of tiny cut up pieces of multi-coloured wire beneath it.

'Did a good job, didn't I?' Dad's standing behind me with his tea in his hand. 'The commander stood on the stairs and watched me, he didn't think I could do it, but I showed him. Took me a while but I showed him.'

'Who's the commander Dad?'

'MI5 Commander. Orders from the top.'

'Why dismantle the phone?'

'To stop *them* from listening in. They can tap

92

phones you know. I've done all of the phone sockets in the house and next I'm doing the electric sockets because they can tap those too, although not many people know that.'

'You can't do that Dad, you'll electrocute yourself.'

'Oh, you've no need to worry, I'm protected. They protect me.' He pats me on the arm. 'Because they've told me.' He leans closer and whispers, 'I'm special. That's why I've been chosen.'

This is so much worse. And I thought he was getting better.

'Well, you've obviously had a busy night Dad, sit down and I'll pour you another cup of tea.' We go back into the kitchen.

'Okay, one more won't hurt I suppose.' he settles himself at the table.

I take my phone out of my pocket and text Nick:
Emergency call me now

He rings almost immediately, 'Hello Lou, what's up?' I can tell by the echo that he's on hands free in his car.

'Need to talk to you,' I shout, 'where are you?'

'On my way to yours, thought I'd surprise you. Should be with you in about half an hour.'

Thank God for that.

'I'm at Dad's. Bit of a situation, can you come here instead?'

'What's wrong? What's happened?'

'I'll explain when you get here. Can you do me a favour on the way? You've still got my house key, haven't you?'

'Yeah, Why?'

'Can you call in at mine and pick Sprocket up and take him to Linda's for me?'

'Yeah, sure. Text me her address. Are you okay?'

'I'm fine.' No, I'm not. 'Just hurry up and get here.'

I hang up and text him Linda's address then text Linda asking her to have Sprocket and that I'll explain later.

I persuade Dad to come into the lounge and wait for Nick to arrive before we clear his bedroom of furniture. He's agreed and is settled in his armchair watching a house makeover programme.

It's clear to me that we can't leave Dad on his own anymore; Nick and I will have to take turns in staying here overnight and we're going to have to sort something out for the daytime too.

I'm going to ring the Mental Health team first thing on Monday morning and ask for Dad's appointment to be brought forward.

'Turn that up, will you?' Dad barks at me.

'Sorry?'

'Turn it up,' he says, nodding at the television. 'I can't hear it.'

'Oh, okay.' I pick up the remote control and point it at the TV.

'No, not that one, THAT one,' he says pointing at the TV.

'I am,' I say, confused, pointing the remote control.

'NO! Not the television. Turn up that one.'

I look at him blankly. I have no idea what he's talking about.

He looks at me exasperated.

'Turn up the mystery voice.'

'What mystery voice?'

He sighs. 'The mystery voice on the television.

94

Turn it up so I can hear it properly.'

'What's the mystery voice?'

'Sshh....' he flaps his hand at me. 'I can't hear what it's saying.'

Hurry up Nick.

Nick finally arrives an hour after our telephone call. Dad has deteriorated dreadfully; he keeps leaning over the coffee table next to him and talking as if he's having a conversation with someone. Every now and then he'll look over at me and I have the feeling that he's talking about me. I can't make out what he's saying but every so often he'll laugh as if he's heard something funny. He hasn't spoken to me at all since the mystery voice conversation and when I've spoken to him he hasn't answered.

As soon as I hear Nick's car I dash out to the hallway to let him in, so I can fill him in on what's happening.

'I've dropped Sprocket off at Linda's, she seemed a bit chattier this time,' he says with a smile. I close the lounge door behind me, so Dad can't hear us.

'I'm frightened Nick,' I say. 'Dad's so much worse and I don't know what we should do.' I bring him up to date on the morning's events and I can see that he can't quite believe it.

'Is he really so much worse?'

'Yes,' I say, opening the lounge door. 'Don't say I didn't warn you.'

'Hello Dad,' says Nick in a jolly voice as he walks in. 'How are you feeling.'

Dad is talking to the invisible person, but he stops and looks up in surprise.

'Well, hello Commander,' he says getting to his

feet. 'This is a surprise I must say.' Dad salutes Nick.

We can't wait until Monday for help.

I ring the number of the Mental Health team and write down the out of office hours given out on the recording. I'm not hopeful that they're going to be any help on a Saturday but we're desperate. I can hear Nick and Dad's footsteps upstairs and the faint sound of their voices.

I ring the out of hours number and wait, after what seems like an hour but is surely only minutes, a woman answers. I give her Dad's details and patient number.

'How can I help?' she says. I tell her Dad has an appointment for three weeks' time, then I tell her of the events today. She listens without comment then says, 'please hold for a moment.' Five minutes go by and I begin to think I've been cut off when suddenly she's back.

'Okay, Miss Russell. The Mental Health team will be coming out to you today, but I can't give you a time at the moment, but they will be coming. I'm going to give you their mobile number to ring if your father should worsen but if you can be patient they will be with you later.'

Thank God, someone is going to help. I thank her profusely and hang up.

I can hear Nick and Dad coming down the stairs so go out into the hallway.

'I'm going to make some lunch, any requests?' I say in a jolly holly sticks voice.

Nick looks ashen.

'Anything, don't mind,' says Nick. 'Not really hungry.'

'I'll have a ham sandwich if that's okay, Commander?' Dad looks at Nick with his eyebrows raised. Nick just nods. I don't think he can speak. At least Dad seems to be hearing what I'm saying now.

I make sandwiches and tea and take them through to the lounge; Dad tucks into his with relish while Nick and I pick at ours. I wonder how long we'll have to wait and more importantly, I wonder what can they do?

They've arrived. The Mental Health team consists of two men, one sporty type in a tracksuit called Geoff and a tall man who I think is a doctor. We're standing in the hallway and I'm updating them on Dad's condition.

It's now six o'clock and the afternoon seemed to go on forever. Dad stopped talking to the coffee table and started to take an interest in what was going on outside.

'Look at them,' he said, pointing out of the window. 'See all those people sat on my car. I'm going to go and sort them out.' We looked, we really did, as if what he was saying was real. He got more and more agitated and annoyed, said they were guerrillas and that *they* had sent them to make him give up his mission.

We tried to persuade him to stay indoors but short of physically restraining him what could we do? We went outside with him and he could still see them and started shouting at them and waving his arms. Simon from next door came out to ask if everything was alright. He seemed really concerned and tried to talk to Dad, but Dad didn't recognise him; looked right through him as if he wasn't even there. We thanked

Simon for his concern and told him it would be better if he went back inside, said we were waiting for the doctor. I think he was relieved and we didn't need to tell him twice. I don't think he could quite believe the way Dad was, I couldn't either. We tried to humour Dad but in the end Nick pretended he was the Commander and ordered him to go back inside and wait for orders. Dad looked crestfallen and meekly walked inside muttering that he was only trying to complete his mission.

It was heart-breaking, and he just got worse and worse. He got really agitated and wouldn't sit down even when Nick ordered him to in his guise as the commander. He was pacing the room and talking to himself and other people who weren't there. He ignored us.

He looked dreadful, pale and sweating and I thought if he carried on like it his heart would give out and he'd die. At about four o'clock I said, 'why don't you have a rest Dad? Have a break.' I thought he'd ignore me, but he brushed his hand over his head and said, 'yes, I think I will. It's going to be a long night.'

Nick and I steered him to the sofa and laid him down and put a throw over him. He closed his eyes and we thought he'd gone to sleep. Then he started singing.

'So,' says Geoff, 'from what you say we're probably going to have to admit him. Do you think he'd come willingly?'

'I don't know.' I say.

'I think he will,' says Nick, 'if I pretend I'm his commander and tell him to.'

'It would be much better if he comes willingly,'

says Philip, 'otherwise we'll need to wait for another doctor, so we can section him.'

Section him. Oh my God, section him. I can't quite take it in.

'Okay, let's go and talk to him.'

They go through to the lounge; Dad is lying on the sofa. He's asleep, well he has his eyes closed. But he's singing, the same song over and over again. 'The sunny side of the street.'

'TOM,' Geoff is talking loudly to him. 'TOM, CAN YOU HEAR ME?'

Philip gently shakes Dad's arm, but Dad continues to sing and doesn't answer. They continue trying to rouse him but after ten minutes we're all back in the hallway.

'Okay, he's not in a coherent state to give his permission so we're going to need another doctor to section him. Are you okay with that? Philip looks at me and Nick.

What choice do we have?

'Yes,' we both say. 'What do you think is wrong with him?' I ask Philip, 'What's wrong with our Dad?'

He's quiet for a moment, thinking. 'Obviously we can't make a diagnosis without tests but from what I've seen I would say he's having a psychotic episode.'

'What could have caused it?' asks Nick, 'Will he get better?'

'Many things can cause it but without further investigation I can't say anymore at the moment; the important thing is that we get him into hospital where we can help him and find out what's going on.' He takes out his mobile. 'I'm going to ring for another doctor and an ambulance. Hopefully we won't have to wait too long.'

We follow the ambulance in Nick's car. We don't talk, I think we're both in a state of shock. They're taking Dad to the Elderly Mental Health Unit which is in a separate building within the hospital grounds. I'm nervous, I have visions of a Victorian lunatic asylum with people banging on doors shouting to be let out. I'm being ridiculous.

I hope.

They've taken Dad round to the back entrance, but we have to go in through the visitor's entrance, so we follow the signs and park the car. I tramp across to the ticket machine which of course is broken so I go back to the car.

'I'll walk round to the main car park and get a ticket.'

'Don't bother,' says Nick. 'I don't care if I get a fine.'

'No, I'll get one,' I say, starting to walk off.

'Don't bother,' Nick shouts after me. 'I don't fucking care if I get a ticket. Just leave it.'

He's right, of course he's right. I stop and walk back, and we head towards the *Blossom Unit.*

'Sorry. Wasn't having a go at you.'

'I know, forget it. Doesn't matter. You're right.'

'I just can't believe this, it's like some fucking nightmare and I can't wake up.'

'It's worse than a nightmare.'

'Everything's turning to shit,' Says Nick.

It is.

The Blossom Unit is an ordinary building – which is a relief. We have to press a buzzer and wait. After a few minutes a disembodied voice asks us to step in front of the camera. It's only then that we notice a camera lens over the door; we step forward. Moments later there's another buzz and the door clicks open.

We follow the sign to 'Reception'. It's very quiet. No screaming.

We then press another buzzer and are let into *Bluebell Ward*. It looks like a regular hospital ward except that the nurses' station is in a booth with windows and a door with a keypad lock on it. It's in the middle of a large room with sofas and occasional tables scattered around. An elderly lady is sitting in an armchair by the window knitting what looks like longest scarf in the world, an elderly man is trudging in slow shuffling steps around the nurses' station.

A smiling woman introduces herself as Sister Kathy although she's dressed in normal clothing, not a nurse's uniform. She gently steers the shuffling man over to the windows and he continues to shuffle in smaller circles then she comes back over to us, a practiced smile on her face.

'You must be Tom's family. Come through.'

She unlocks the booth door by tapping in a code and we go in. A couple of desks and masses of files and boxes are crammed into a very small space. A bank of television screens, all showing the insides of bedrooms, look down at us from the walls. Kathy moves files and boxes from two chairs and we wedge ourselves into the seats.

'Now, while we get Tom settled in we just need to go through a few things.' She notices the shell-shocked look on our faces. 'Try not to worry,' she says, 'he's in the right place now, he's safe.'

We're very lucky I know. Mental health beds are like gold dust, we are extremely fortunate that there was one bed free for Dad otherwise he could have been sent miles away.

'Let me tell you a little about the unit. We have only twelve patients at a time and everyone has their own room and bathroom. We've tried to make it has unlike a hospital as possible but obviously we can only go so far. All of our patients are older adults, most of them are past retirement age.'

She opens a file and we go through everything that's happened today and she makes copious notes.

'Okay, I just need to check with the staff how your father's settling in, but I won't be long.'

She leaves the office and shuts the door.

'Is that to keep us in or them out?' says Nick grimly.

'Probably both.'

'Can we see him?' Nick asks when she returns.

'Not at the moment, but he's fine don't worry. He's still asleep and in bed but we've taken his obs and he's fine. Once he's awake we'll start some more detailed investigations. The best thing you can do is go home and come back tomorrow.'

I wanted to see him, make sure he's okay. He won't know where he is when he wakes up.

'Look,' says Kathy reaching up to one of the screens and flicking the switch. 'He's fine, fast asleep.'

The screen flickers to life to show Dad tucked up in bed like a child with the covers pulled up to his neck and his arms tucked in.

He's still singing.

Chapter Eight

'At least he's safe,' I say.

'That's right. He's in the right place.' Nick nods thoughtfully.

'They can help him there.'

We're trying to convince ourselves; trying to make ourselves feel better. We've just left Dad incarcerated in a secure mental unit and we're not feeling good about it. He's a prisoner. We're parked outside my house sitting in the car and are going to walk round to Linda's to pick up Sprocket. It's a beautiful evening, very warm for June. There's a light breeze and it's still light although it's half past eight. The weather feels like a traitor, it should be stormy, bleak and miserable to match our moods.

'We'd better paste a smile on our faces before we inflict ourselves on Linda,' I say as we arrive at her door and ring the bell.

'Easy for me, I do it all of the time.'

'Helloo.' We fix smiles as she opens the door, she looks at us a bit funny and I think our rictus grins might have frightened her. She lets us in and Sprocket hurls himself at me and nearly knocks me over.

'Come on into the dining room,' Linda says. 'I've done us some supper – I know it's late, but I bet you haven't eaten.'

I'm about to say that I'm not hungry but the smell

of garlic sets my mouth watering.

'Don't want to put you to any trouble.' Nick gives her a model-man smile.

'No trouble at all.' Linda pulls the chairs out from the table in the dining room. 'Sit yourselves down and I'll bring it in. It's nothing special but it'll fill a gap.'

She bustles out to the kitchen and comes back in with a large dish of lasagne which she places in the middle of the table. She goes out again then comes back with garlic bread and salad.

'Okay,' she says, putting them in the middle of the table, 'help yourselves.'

We load our plates up and tuck in; it's delicious.

'This is amazing,' Nick says through his third mouthful 'I didn't realise how hungry I was.'

Linda smiles and pours us all a large glass of red and we chomp in silence. When we've finished I can't believe how much better I feel and I can tell from looking at Nick that he feels the same. We fill Linda in on the day's events and she listens sympathetically.

'Sounds like you were lucky to get a bed at this mental health place.' Linda opens another bottle of red.

'We were,' I say. 'The doctor said some people have to travel a couple of hours to visit their relatives. Imagine that.'

'Nightmare. That lasagne was *so* good. Shouldn't really have had second helpings. Got to watch the waistline.' Nick pats his stomach. 'If I can't fit into the samples they'll get someone else.' He pulls a face.

'Yes, it's a hard life being a top model,' I joke.

'I'm sure it's not as easy as it looks,' Linda says. 'I mean you have to look after your looks and everything.'

'I'm not going to pretend it's rocket science but there is a skill to it like everything else and you're always looking over your shoulder at the competition. There's an assumption that if you're good looking it's an accident of birth and you're lucky. Which is true, but really, it's no different from being born a genius, that's an accident of birth too but no-one dismisses geniuses as being born lucky. There's respect if you're clever but not if you have a pretty face.'

'That's very profound, Nick, hope you're not expecting sympathy.' I nudge him.

'Was a bit deep wasn't it? Plenty of time to think when you're pouting and posing. And I definitely wasn't expecting sympathy from you.' He laughs. 'Anyway, I'll be downgraded to catalogue work soon – too old and not the right *look*.'

'Look?' says Linda.

'The up and coming models who do well have a look, a trademark. They don't even have to be good looking. One guy you've probably seen has tats everywhere, even on his head.'

'Yeah, I've seen him,' says Linda. 'Always looking moody and miserable, never smiles, shaved head, very muscled and toned.'

'He is, great gym honed physique,' says Nick, 'and the reason he never smiles or shows his teeth is because he hasn't got any.'

'No teeth!'

'Well he's got a few but they're rotten, makes you feel sick when he smiles. Black stumps. He's only 23.'

'You liar.' I laugh.

He laughs too. 'Honestly, it's true. They've booked him for the Christmas shoot I'm doing on Monday for Next. He's doing the edgy teenager stuff.'

'A Christmas shoot in June, really?'

'Yep,' Nick says getting up from the table. 'You think you decide what to wear but you don't, it's all been decided six months in advance for you.' He pauses. 'Although probably not for you Linda, you've got your own style, sort of retro. I like it.'

He's right, Linda's wearing a plum coloured, flowery long dress with smocking around the middle and smocking around the neck. Looks seventies to me. I'd feel self-conscious wearing it but it looks great on her. I feel quite dull by comparison in my Next summer dress.

'Thanks.' She's blushing.

It's quite late when we leave but we're in much better moods that when we arrived. We've all had a bit too much wine and I'm ready for bed. We offer to help clear up, but Linda won't hear of it. I feel a bit guilty leaving her to do it all, but I feel absolutely done in, so I don't protest too much.

I hug Linda. 'Thank you so much, tonight's really done us good.'

Nick kisses Linda on the cheek. 'It has, thank you for a wonderful meal, Linda, see you soon.'

I sneak a look at Linda's face as we're leaving.

I've seen that look before.

Smitten.

We stand outside Blossom Unit waiting to be buzzed in.

'It's like a prison,' says Nick, smiling for the camera.

'It is,' I say out of the corner of my mouth. We're buzzed in and the door releases.

Yet another locked door; we're buzzed into the

ward and in we go. It's stifling inside, definitely no air-con in here. The temperature must be hitting thirty degrees today but tomorrow there may be a frost, typical British weather.

'Christ, the music's enough to send you round the bend,' says Nick quietly.

I know what he means, I don't know if it's the radio or a CD but it reminds me of the black and white minstrel show that was always on when I was very little. Songs from the musicals sung by people who can't sing. Blacked up men with white chalky mouths.

I spot Dad straight away. He's sitting in an armchair by the window, he has a newspaper on his lap which he's not reading because he's listening to the knitting woman sitting next to him.

As we get closer I can see that the scarf she's knitting is even longer than yesterday and I also realise that although her mouth is moving she's saying the same words over and over, knit, purl, knit, purl...

'Hello.' Dad has spotted us and gives us a big smile. He's smartly dressed in a shirt and trousers and I'm glad that we had the presence of mind to bring a bag of his clothes with us last night.

We say our hellos and Nick asks Dad how he's feeling.

'Oh, can't complain. They're very nice here you know. And it's been nice talking to my Betty again. She's looking out for me you know, says she's going to visit soon.'

He's talking to Mum now.

Nick and I exchange worried glances as he finds us a couple of chairs and we pull them over in front of Dad and settle ourselves.

'Hello.' A uniformed woman appears and introduces herself. 'I'm nursing assistant Liz, but I'm also the family assistance co-ordinator. I can help with any leaflets and organisations you might need to contact. If Thomas should need anything or you're not sure of anything, then just let me know and I'll do what I can to help.'

Irrationally, I decide that I don't like her; it's Tom not Thomas. She's also looking at Nick the whole time she's speaking which is not unusual but for Christ's sake this is a mental hospital. Show some restraint. And respect.

'So,' she says turning to Dad, 'are you going to introduce me to your visitors?'

Dad looks at her and then Nick, and says, 'This is my son Nick.'

'Hello, Nick,' she says fluttering her eyelashes at Nick. 'Nice to meet you. And who is this lady here?' She says to Dad waving a hand in my direction.

Dad looks at me but doesn't say anything.

Liz opens her mouth to speak and I want to tell her to shut up and go away and mind her own business. Everything is happening in slow motion and I'm powerless to stop it, but I know what he's going to say, and I don't want him to.

'Thomas? Who is this lovely lady, is she your daughter?'

Dad looks at her in surprise. 'Oh no. She's not my daughter. I don't know who she is.'

'Lou, he's not well. Of course he knows who you are.'

We walk across the car park back to the car. I don't know how I got through the visit. I plastered a

108

fake smile on my face and pretended everything was fine; I was pleasant to Liz when really I wanted to punch her in the face. I chatted to Dad, but he more or less ignored me. As if I wasn't there.

'He doesn't. He doesn't have a clue who I am. He knew who you were though. I'm obviously forgettable.' My voice is thick, I feel like I'm choking.

I'm also disgusted with myself for making it all about me. Dad's ill and I know he's not in his right mind but a childish, brattish part of me just keeps on asking why does he know Nick but not me? Does he love Nick more? Has he always just tolerated me? It's not fair, a childish part of me cries.

I know I'm being ridiculous and Dad can't help it, but it hurts.

'He's very confused – he's in a strange place with strange people. Remember he thought I was the commander so he didn't know who I was either.'

'I know. Ignore me, I'm just being pathetic. 'It's probably the weather. It's too hot.'

'Too hot? We've had a couple of days of sunshine and you're moaning it's too hot. You'll be saying we need rain next. Anyway, just forget about it, I'm sure next time we go he'll know who you are.'

Why does it matter so much? I give myself a mental slap. Dad's ill and the important thing is that he gets better.

'Sounds like they have lots planned for tomorrow,' says Nick, changing the subject.

They do, x-ray of Dad's head to make sure there's no physical injury that could be causing his symptoms, MRI scan and assorted blood and urine tests. He'll also be seen by a psychiatrist. It is a relief now he's in there and being looked after, no more worrying about nocturnal outings or the possibility of electrocuting himself. He even showed us his room, or rather he showed Nick, I just trailed along behind them. It wasn't too bad, it had a bed, wardrobe, desk and chair. They said we could bring his television in if we like, there was an aerial socket. He even had his own bathroom.

We spoke to his appointed nurse on our way out, out of Dad's earshot. He's called Gus, he seemed very gentle and sort of unhurried. He said he helped Dad to get dressed this morning and helped him to shave which I thought was a bit strange as Dad's always managed on his own. He's always looked well turned out and clean shaven when I've visited him, and he never had anyone to help him at home.

'He doesn't seem to mind being in there,' Nick goes on, 'which surprises me 'cos I never thought he'd leave his house willingly.'

'Nor me,' I say, 'talking of which we'd better let Jean know that she doesn't need to go to Dad's tomorrow. I'll ring her later. You know she'll want to visit Dad. What should I tell her?'

'The sister said just us two for the time being while Dad's settling in, so you'd better put her off.'

'She won't like it.'

No she won't but that's too bad. I haven't really forgiven her for that accusing look. I'll drop you off then I'm going to get back to London.'

'Okay, no worries.'

'Sorry I can't stay longer but I've got a job tomorrow. I'll be back either Friday night or Saturday morning.'

'Well I think Dad will be in there a while. I asked sister how long patients usually stay and she said as long as they need to. She said the one in Dad's room before him had been in there for four months.'

'Christ. Hope they can get Dad better quicker than that.'

'If they can make him better. If he doesn't get worse.'

'That's it, Lou. Look on the bright side.'

'Sorry,' I say glumly.

'Come on Lou, buck up. We've got to stay positive or you know what'll happen?'

'What?'

'We'll end up in there with him.'

Nick goes back to London in torrential rain; we hadn't even got back to my house before it began. Big, fat raindrops that quickly turned into a downpour.

'See,' said Nick, 'you wished that on us with your whinging.' He was only joking though. I think.

I'm looking out of the living room window waiting for it to stop then I'm going to take Sprocket out for a walk as he's bouncing around the room being hyper-dog. Nick seems to have that effect on him. Might call for Linda on the way too.

'Hey, what're all those people doing up there?'

There's a small crowd of people milling around at the opening to the Rise. We tramp across the churned-up field sploshing through the mud in our wellies.

'There's a tape across – is there some sort of race on? I don't remember hearing anything about a race or marathon.'

'Crap weather for it,' says Linda.

As we get closer I can see that the tape is blue and has writing on it.

'It's not a race,' I say, walking a bit faster, 'that's police tape.'

We join the crowd of people behind the *Police – do not cross* tape which is stretched right across the entrance to the field.

I hop around trying to see above their heads but can't get a clear view as heads keep bobbing around in the way. I see two police cars parked on the grass and a large white van is pulling up next to them. The ground is already like a mud bath with all the people sloshing around and churning it up. Two policemen are patrolling alongside the tape making sure no-one crosses, their smart uniform trousers plastered in mud.

'Hey officer! Can you tell us what's going on?' someone shouts.

'Stay behind the tape please,' is the only response.

'Isn't that the Truth over there?' says Linda, 'Look. Over there by the trees?'

I look over to where Linda's pointing and see a dejected looking Truth standing under a tree, talking to a policeman. Lulu is trotting around them in an agitated fashion, jumping up at the Truth every so often.

'It is. Wonder what's he doing there?'

The policeman has his hand on Norman's shoulder and is talking to him; Norman has his hand over his mouth and keeps shaking his head.

A murmur ripples through the crowd and everyone watches as two men emerge from the white van carrying a large white package. They walk past Norman and into the trees and undergrowth on the edge of the Rise.

'That's a tent,' says a loud voice, 'Look!'

It is indeed a tent, not with guy ropes though, more an instant pop up tent. A white, square tent. The sort of tent they put over bodies.

Another car pulls up, a large unmarked black car.

A square shaped WPC gets out of the driver's side and a tall man, who I recognise as Detective Inspector Peters, gets out of the passenger door and they make their way over to the white tent.

'Looks like the big guns have arrived,' says Linda.

'That's the one that interviewed me at work.'

Linda narrows her eyes to get a better look. 'He looks a bit like Bryan Ferry.'

The crowd surges forward to look and a man to the side of me nearly knocks me over.

Six-foot-tall, bald, wearing a grubby white T shirt stretched over a bulging gut, all topped off with 'Shamus' tattooed in the middle of a roll of fat on the back of his neck.

I hear a noise and look down to see a nasty looking Jack Russell growling and snarling at Sprocket. Sprocket looks at him for a moment, blinks, then ignores him.

'Shut up, you little fucker,' snaps Shamus, whipping the lead towards himself. The Jack Russell's eyes bulge for a moment; it draws a rasping breath when the choker chain releases.

I catch Linda's eye. 'Shall we move further down?'

She nods, and we detach ourselves and move further down the police tape, away from the main crowd, away from bulging neck Shamus.

'He was nice, wasn't he?'

'Lovely. Frogham's finest. Glad you stood your

ground though Sprocket.' A mud splattered Sprocket looks up at me at the mention of his name. He's going to need a bath when we get home.

'They're arresting him!' shouts Shamus. 'Always knew he was a fucking weirdo!'

A sort of jeering goes up from the crowd as we watch Norman being escorted to a police car. He gets into the back of the car and Lulu jumps up after him. The WPC gets in the front but then the rear door flies opens, and Norman almost falls out. We watch as he vomits all over his own feet. More shouts go up from the crowd, although I can't make out what they're saying.

'Christ it's like a lynch mob,' I say. 'Poor Norman, as if he'd harm a fly.'

'Norman?' Linda looks at me with raised eyebrows.

'Long story, tell you about it sometime.'

The jeering has now grown to shouts of 'weirdo' and 'paedo' amongst other things.

We watch Norman wipe his shoes on the grass then he gets back into the car and is driven off.

'Eew, bet it's not very pleasant in there,' says Linda pulling a face. 'Although I'm pretty sure if you were being arrested they wouldn't let you take your dog with you in the police car.'

'Course they wouldn't,' I nod towards Shamus who seems to be leading the shouting, 'but you can't educate pork.'

A chant of 'paedo, paedo' being led by Shamus is now gaining strength and volume, he's stomping around, fist pumping the air and his face is getting redder and redder.

Two PCs make their way over to Shamus and start

talking to him, I can hear him shouting at them and watch as he jabs a finger in one of the PC's chest. In one swift movement the PC draws his baton and has the baton across Shamus's throat while the other PC has grabbed Shamus's arm and twisted it up his back. I must admit that I'm impressed with the speedy response. A brief struggle plays out which ends with Shamus screaming about police brutality before being marched across the field to a police car. As he's shoved non-too gently into the back of the police car he shouts to his tall skinny mate who's holding the Jack Russell's lead, to look after his dog.

'See, they didn't let him take his dog.' Linda smirks.

We watch as he's driven off. His skinny mate also watches and as the police car disappears from sight he drops the dog lead in the mud and wanders off. The Jack Russell stands still for a moment sniffing the air then trots off after him dragging the lead behind him.

With their ringleader gone the crowd begins to break up and wander off leaving just a handful who linger and move closer to the police tape. I spot a familiar figure heading towards the white police van.

'Hey Rupert!' I call, 'over here!'

Rupert turns and comes towards us.

'Hello Louise,' he booms, 'and this is?' He looks at Linda.

'Hi, I'm Linda, nice to meet you.'

'Charmed m'dear, charmed.' Rupert almost bows. 'Now then ladies, can you fill me in on what's going on.'

'We were hoping you could tell us Rupert,' I say. 'How did you hear about this? This isn't your neck of the woods.'

'I have my sources, that's all I can say. Now, I hear that someone found a body when they were walking their dog.' He lowers his voice and moves closer. 'Apparently, the heavy rain washed the soil away and the dog got hold of a shoe and tried to drag it out of the ground.'

Poor Norman. He's not having much luck; no wonder he was sick.

'Do you know who it is?' Please don't let it be Glenda.

'No, the police are being very tight lipped. But I'm guessing it's the missing woman, the first one. From what I can glean from my source the body's quite decomposed, so she must have been dead for a while.' He roots around in his jacket pocket and produces a Dictaphone. 'Going to see what I can get out of the local plod – no doubt there'll be a press conference tomorrow morning, but I like to get a head start.'

'That Detective Inspector Peters is in the tent,' I say.

'Is he? Hmm, interesting. Maybe I'll renew our acquaintance.'

Rupert buttons his jacket up and attempts to smooth his thick white hair back. 'Wish me luck ladies.' He winks and tramps across the field splashing mud everywhere.

'He's very charming – not how I imagined a reporter to be.'

I laugh. 'No he's not, but that's his secret weapon. He is a sweetheart though, he does actually have scruples, unlike Ralph.'

'But seriously, if it's that missing woman, how awful. I hope Glenda's okay.'

'It doesn't bear thinking about. Someone here in Frogham is a murderer or maybe even a serial killer. Makes you think doesn't it?

'It does. I often come up here on my own and walk Henry, but I don't think I will anymore. Not until they catch this nutter anyway.'

'Nor me.' I shudder.

'Let's go home,' says Linda. 'Come to mine and we'll do a double dog bath. Get the mud off these dirty hounds.'

Sprocket and Henry turn their muddy faces towards us and sniff.

They know.

Chapter Nine

There's a buzz of excitement in the office; at last, some actual real news to put in the paper. Shame that someone had to die for it.

'So,' says Ralph, sucking on a pencil, 'it's definitely that Suzanne woman?'

'Yes Ralph the police issued a statement this morning, she's been formally identified. Apparently,' Rupert continues, 'she had to be identified by dental records which is why it's taken so long. At least her parents have been spared identifying her.'

'Poor cow. Do they know how she died?'

'Post Mortem inconclusive, have to do more tests. Might be a while.'

'Horrible.' Lucy shudders. 'Where has she been all these weeks?'

'God knows, whoever did it must have hidden her somewhere.' I feel quite sick – what if the same fate awaits Glenda?

'I heard some weirdo with a dog found her, is that right?' asks Ian.

Rupert consults his notebook, 'Norman Shuttleworth, age 53, single.'

'He's not a weirdo,' I butt in. 'I know him and he's a very nice man and I'm sure he'd rather not have found her.' I wonder why I'm sticking up for Norman.

'Oh okay. Sorry.' Ian looks a bit shamefaced.

'I wanted to get an interview with him, but the police have told him not to speak about what he found. If we don't get anything else, we'll just have to run with what we've got.'

'Hmm, so as you know him Louise – do you reckon he'd talk to you? Off the record? We could quote you as an unidentified source.'

I just look at Ralph.

'Oh, Okay, perhaps not. Rupert, keep me posted.' He doesn't even look shamefaced about it.

'Louise, before you sit down can you come into my office for a minute?'

I'm immediately suspicious. The only time I got invited into Ralph's office was when I came for an interview for the job. I follow him and am surprised when he asks me to shut the door. Am I about to get the sack? Cutbacks maybe. Perhaps I should have agreed to speak to the Truth after all.

'Sit yourself down.'

I perch gingerly on the threadbare swivel chair and await my fate, must be the sack.

'Right then girl, do you want to tell me what's going on?' Ralph says munching on a boiled sweet. Not very PC, is he? *Girl*, honestly.

'There's nothing going on that I know of.'

'Don't give me that. You've been as miserable as sin and something's wrong and I want to know what it is. You look like you're not eating either. It's not the job is it? You're not thinking of leaving, are you? Because it goes without saying that I don't want you to leave but I can't afford to give you a pay rise.'

I was going to give the stock answer that nothing is wrong but somehow, I find myself telling him. All of it. Dad, MI5, the lot.

He listens without comment then draws a deep breath. 'I wish you'd told me, we could have helped with time off and stuff. Do you want some time off? Compassionate leave?'

'No thanks, I'd rather be here to be honest, I'll only brood at home.'

'Okay, but if you change your mind you only have to ask. Now, no more bottling it up -you need anything, you ask. Right?'

Feeling unexpectedly choked at his concern I fight to stay composed.

'Yes, I will,' I say in a very small voice.

'My old mum went mental,' he goes on, 'fucking awful it was, wouldn't wish it on my worst enemy. I know what you're going through and the only advice I can give is don't be too hard on yourself.'

'Thanks Ralph.' I get up to leave. 'How is your mum now?'

'She died a couple of years back.' He looks down at the desk. 'Was a blessing really, her last few years were pretty awful, not just for her but for us as well. But do you know what the worst thing was? At the end she didn't even know her own face in the mirror and I prayed for her to die. But when she did I was devastated. I didn't care that she didn't know who I was, I just wanted her not to be dead. I thought I'd be relieved, but I wasn't.'

'Oh, Ralph, I'm so sorry.'

He won't look at me and says gruffly, 'Go on, get back to work, I'm not running a bleeding charity y'know.'

I knew there was a heart in there somewhere.

'Salt and vinegar?'

'No thanks.'

Maria expertly wraps six portions of chips and puts them in a plastic bag.

'You all got the munchies today?'

I laugh. 'I think we have. Thanks Maria.'

It probably says something about my diet that I'm on first name terms with the chip shop owner. I quick march back to the office before the chips go cold, the smell of them tormenting me. I decided to treat myself to a bag of chips for lunch and of course everyone else wanted some too. On my way in I nearly collide with Lev who's coming out of the office in a hurry.

'Oh, Lev, didn't see you there, you made me jump.'

'Is bill, put on your desk.' he mumbles, keeping his head down. He has a baseball cap on and doesn't seem to want to look at me.

'Okay, thanks.'

He puts a hand up and pulls his hat lower.

'You okay Lev?'

Before he can answer Ian shouts from the office.

'Hey Lev, what you done to your face? Been in a fight?'

Lev is forced to turn around to answer him, which gives me a better view of his face.

'No, is my cat, is vicious basterd.' He pulls the cap lower, but it doesn't hide the four deep scratches down one side of his face. They're more like gouges than scratches and are crusty with blood. He puts his head down and hurries down the stairs without saying anything more.

'Didn't look like cat scratches to me,' says Ian as I

121

put his chips on his desk. 'Looked more like fingernail marks.'

'Ian,' Lucy admonishes, 'you shouldn't say things like that.'

Ian shrugs. 'Only telling it how I see it and I can tell you that was no cat. Looked like someone has raked their fingers down his face.'

'You don't know that, you only got a glimpse of him.'

'Exactly. If it was a cat why's he trying to hide them?' He puts a chip in his mouth. 'Christ these are hot.'

'Yeah, that's on account of them just being cooked?'

He holds his mouth open to cool the chip. 'There's no salt on these is there?'

'In the kitchen.' I put Lucy's chips on her desk.

'You going in there? Could you bring it back with you?'

I'm not visiting Dad tonight; I tell myself it's because I already have something else arranged but I don't want to go to that either.

I don't want to see Dad; there, I've admitted it.

The visit on Monday and last night was okay, Dad seemed pleased to see me, but he doesn't know who I am. On Monday I asked him if he knew who I was, and he just looked at me. I asked him if he thought I was family and he said, 'Oh, no, I don't think so.' After more questioning it turns out he thinks I'm a nurse, but he was getting a bit upset, as if he knew he should remember but couldn't. I felt ashamed of myself for asking him and I'm not going to ask him again.

Last night he started talking about mum. He thinks he's in a hotel and mum's going to be joining him soon, he's been talking to her over the radio. He was quite excited about it and was looking forward to seeing her. I started to get upset then and he patted my hand and asked why was I crying?

'We're going to have a lovely holiday. Your mother's really looking forward to seeing you.' When I left he gave me a hug. 'Drive carefully, Louise.' He knew who I was then, just for a while.

Anyway, I'm not going tonight and I'm using the excuse that I have to go to Linda's clairvoyant night. I don't want to go to that either but if I don't I'll have to go and visit Dad.

Getting changed out of my work clothes, Ralph's comment comes back to me about looking like I'm not eating. Come to think of it my jeans feel quite loose and a month ago they were quite snug. I decide to weigh myself and hunt the scales out from under the bed where they were banished to a long time ago.

I blow the dust off them and switch them on. I remove my jeans, bra and pants and the hair slide out of my hair too. Then take my watch off as that probably weighs a pound or two. I get on the scales and am pleasantly surprised when I see that I've lost about ten pounds. Ten pounds in less than three weeks; there is an upside to being miserable. My meals have been just the same but thinking about it I have been leaving food on my plate. Apart from the chips at lunchtime; I didn't leave any of those.

Sprocket comes in and waddles over and sniffs the scales, he's looking a bit podgy so has obviously been hovering up the leftovers. I get dressed again and take a look at myself in the mirror; yep, a definite improvement. Feeling ridiculously pleased with myself I shut a howling Sprocket in the kitchen and leave the house.

Apart from the medium I'm the last to arrive at Linda's, five people are settled cosily in the lounge waiting to contact the dead. I only said I'd come to make up the numbers. Linda's really into the spiritual scene and quite often has Sally the medium round; she's been trying to get me to come for ages and she caught me in a weak moment. Already regretting it I stump up my ten pounds and sit down next to Linda.

Sally arrives in a flurry of chiffon scarves and jangly beads, her blonde and grey shaggy hair making her look like a nervous afghan hound.

'So sorry I'm late my dears, I was just getting into the car and a lady in spirit insisted on getting in with me. We had quite a chat and she was very eager to come through to one of you here tonight.'

What a load of old cobblers.

A dining chair is placed in the centre of the room facing us and she settles herself down in a cloud of patchouli oil. The room isn't that big, and our knees are nearly touching hers, it all feels claustrophobic and stifling.

'I'll just give you an idea of what's going to happen.'

The room is quiet, everyone except me is hanging on her every word.

'People in spirit send their messages through me, I have no control over what they say and sometimes it can be a bit vague as they're not always as clear as I would like. Sometimes they'll have a message for someone which might not make sense at the time but will later. Not everyone will get a message but don't take it personally. Spirits can be quite shy! So,' she says, scanning our faces, 'shall we begin?'

Everyone nods enthusiastically. Except for me.

Sally closes her eyes and takes a deep breath in through her nose; her bracelets jangle. The room holds its breath.

'I'm getting a name.'

Her voice sounds a bit quivering, is it because of the length of the journey from the other side? I stifle a giggle.

'Does the name Judith mean anything to anyone?'

Silence. No one speaks.

'Joyce? Joan?' a grey-haired lady with pearls shows a flicker of recognition and Sally pounces.

'And what's your name?'

'Anne.'

'Anne, is your mother in spirit? Is her name Joan?'

'My mother's dead but her name's not Joan.'

Sally makes a noise which sounds like a tut to me. She breaths in deeply through her nose and fixes Anne with an intense gaze.

'Although I had an auntie called Joan,' Anne says uncertainly.

'Ah, yes,' says Sally, 'but she was like a mother to you, wasn't she?'

'Um...'

'She's telling me about some keys.' Sally looks up to the ceiling. 'They're in a drawer in a sideboard. Does that mean anything to you dear?'

'Um, not that I can think of...' She looks apologetic that it doesn't mean anything.

Sally looks at the ceiling again. 'Yes, Joan I'll tell

her.' She looks at Anne. 'Joan says you need to find the keys in the sideboard and when you find them you'll know what to do.' She looks heavenward again. 'Okay, God Bless.' Sally fixes Anne with a smile. 'She's gone now. It may not mean anything to you yet but take that with you and I promise that it will all make sense.'

Sally swiftly moves on and the next spirit to come through is someone's father, then someone's sister, then a cat called Billy. They all have messages and if it doesn't make sense they're told to 'take that with you'. As far as I can see no-one has heard anything that means anything to them. Having trouble keeping a straight face I'm fighting to stop myself from looking up to the ceiling to see who's there.

There won't be a message for me, I'm quite sure of that. Sally's quite clever at reading people and getting information out them but I'm very good at not giving anything away, other than that I think this is hokum.

We eventually break for wine and nibbles. How can I make an early getaway without upsetting Linda? Listening to the conversation it seems that the more everyone talks about their *messages* the more convinced they become that a loved one is talking to them.

'Enjoying yourself?' Linda hands me a glass of wine.

'Yes, it's really interesting. Not what I was expecting.' A complete lie but I don't want to upset her.

'Maybe you'll get a message in the second half.'

'Mmm.'

'Sheila can't believe it.' Sheila is Linda's neighbour from across the road. 'She says there's no way that

Sally could possibly have known her cat was called Billy or how much he meant to her. I think she's feeling a bit spooked.'

'Yes, it's uncanny.' I take a glug of wine. Billy started off as 'does anyone know a William?' and Sally finally arrived at Billy after a lot of prompting and leading questions. Apparently, Billy the cat is looking after Sheila from the other side.

I watch Sally scoffing a sausage roll, her plate is piled high with food and she's on her second glass of alcohol free wine. A free supper plus a tenner a head and she's making a lot of money for an evening's work. Well, hardly work, I reckon anyone could do it if they've got the nerve.

Another refill of wine and we're off again.

'I have a Betty coming through, can anyone take that?'

Silence. I sneak a look out of the corner of my eye; no one is going to take it.

'Betty anyone? She's very insistent – she has a very important message for someone.'

Well if it was that important she'd surely have a name to give it to. I'm determined not to speak.

The others are looking at each other desperately trying to think if they know anyone called Betty. The silence is becoming embarrassing.

'LOUISE!' Sally almost shouts my name and I jump.

'Betty has a message for you – do you know a Betty who's in spirit?'

'Yes.' I'm not going to feed her. I won't tell her my mother was called Betty.

'Betty is very worried for you. She's quite agitated and you need to listen carefully.' Sally looks at me intently. 'Are you listening?' she peers into my eyes earnestly and her beads jangle with the effort, dislodging a flake of pastry from her chiffon scarf.

'Yes,' I say begrudgingly.

'She says there is danger near to you and you must be careful.'

Everyone gasps, except me.

'Betty says,' Sally pauses for dramatic effect, 'that you must be careful who you trust, that people are not what they seem. She sees that you are struggling at the moment, but you must not worry, everything will be alright. But different. She is watching over Tom.'

She somehow has my parent's names, probably from chatting to Linda. I nod thoughtfully as if it means something to me and luckily it seems my turn is over as she turns away, looks up to the ceiling.

'Roger? I have a Roger coming through. He's saying something about a watch in the attic, can anyone take that?'

A tiny, birdlike woman called Moira pipes up. 'I had a great uncle Ronald, he had a fob watch that he always wore.'

Sally turns to her. 'Yes, dear, that's right, it's Ronald. He's telling me about the watch he always wore.'

'Yes, yes he did.' Moira twitters excitedly forgetting that she just told Sally that herself.

'Was the watch lost when he passed? He's saying that the watch is in a trunk in the attic.'

Moira looks confused. 'Oh, I though he left it to my brother...'

'Yes dear, he did,' says Sally firmly, 'but there's another watch and it's in the attic and you must look for it or ask your family if they can look for it.'

Moira looks totally lost now. 'Oh, but...'

'It may not mean anything now but take it with you dear.' She pats Moira on the arm.

She turns to me again. 'Louise,' Betty is being very insistent and won't leave until you listen.'

'I have listened.'

'No. Betty is very insistent. She says that you're not taking her seriously and you must.'

I look at her and try to look as if I believe what she's saying.

'Betty says that Tom is happy in his own way and if it comforts him to think he's in a hotel then where's the harm in that. 'I keep my expression neutral. 'She's been talking to him and she thinks that it's helping him. She wants me to tell you again, there is danger near to you, beware who you trust.' She looks at the ceiling. 'Yes, dear, God Bless.' She focuses on me again. 'It may not mean anything now, dear, but take it with you.'

I don't need to take it with me. I never told anyone about Dad thinking he was in a hotel or that he'd been talking to mum.

Maybe there's something in this clairvoyant malarkey after all.

Since Ralph gave up smoking, most afternoons at about three o'clock he prowls the office like a caged animal. He looks at a few folders here, noses out of the window to see what's going on in the precinct, looks over Ian and Rupert's shoulder to see what they're working on and is generally annoying. Ian says it's his way of releasing the pent-up energy he's built up by not smoking. The first week he did it there were no end of rows but now we just ignore him.

The front door intercom buzzes and as Ralph is on his afternoon prowl he answers it. He presses the buzzer release button and we hear heavy footsteps coming up the stairs.

Detective Inspector Peters comes into the office and a large, stern looking WPC clomps in behind him. Ralph greets them, and they follow him into his office and close the door. After a few minutes there are more footsteps on the stairs and Lev appears in the doorway. He looks furtively around the office then sidles over to Ralph's office, knocks on the door and goes in and closes the door.

They must be quite cosy in there as it's a small office for three men and a woman who's more than a bit on the large side.

We hear raised voices and suddenly Ralph's door is flung open.

'If I no under arrest I no answer questions.' Lev marches out of the office.

Detective Inspector Peters follows him out. 'Mr Dromska, if you could come to the station voluntarily I'm sure we can clear this up in no time.'

Lev swings around and folds his arms defensively, 'Is nothing to clear up. I am going back to work. I told you. Basterd cat scratch me.'

'Would that be *your* cat Mr Dromska?' asks Peters.

Lev looks uncomfortable. 'Er, no. Is cat I see in street. It attack me. Now I go to work.'

'Mr Dromska. I must insist you accompany me to the station.'

'NO! I going back to work.' His face is red, highlighting the scratches.

The Detective Inspector sighs, 'I'm afraid you

leave me no choice. Levi Dromska, I am arresting you on suspicion of kidnapping. You do not have...'

The rest of his words are lost in the kerfuffle as Lev makes an attempt to escape by running towards the stairs. Peters nods at the policewoman who swiftly rugby tackles Lev and wrestles him to the floor with a painful sounding thump. Her mousy square hair doesn't move at all, and as she's twice the size of Lev he doesn't stand a chance.

'No! I done no wrong!' he wails. She ignores him and pins him to the floor with her knee. 'It'll go much easier for you, sir, if you come quietly.' Her voice is gruff. I can't take my eyes off the soles of her shoes; they're enormous and must be at least a size nine. She expertly cuffs him and with a swift movement hauls him to his feet with one hand as if he were a rag doll.

Detective Inspector Peters watches impassively and once Lev is on his feet he nods as she manhandles Lev out of the office and down the stairs.

'Mr Edwards.' The Detective Inspector nods at Ralph. 'We'll be in touch.'

'Righto,' says Ralph. 'By the way, has anyone ever told you that you look just like that Bryan Ferry bloke?'

'No Sir. Never.' He deadpans then turns and heads down the stairs.

'Surprised at that,' says Ralph as he watches him leave. 'Likeness is uncanny.'

Ian suppresses a snigger.

The rest of us are in shock and sit at our desks open mouthed looking at each other. Ralph strides across to the window and, as one, we all jump up and scuttle over to join him.

We watch through the window as Lev is bundled

into the back of the police car, the WPC's large hand expertly holding his head down as she pushes him into the back seat. She walks round to the driver's side, gets in and drives off.

'Fuck me,' says Ralph in disbelief. 'That's a turn up for the books.'

'Kidnapping?' says Lucy. 'Do they mean the murdered woman?'

'Dunno, they were a bit cagey, wouldn't tell me anything but it must be. We don't get many kidnappings around here, do we?'

'Don't they have to have evidence to arrest someone?' I say.

'Would have thought so.'

'I'm sure there's been some sort of mistake,' says Rupert, 'I can't believe Lev has anything to do with it.'

'Well there's no smoke without fire,' says Ian. 'I told you those scratches looked a bit dodge. And he did try to hide them. And he lives around the corner from the dead one and the missing one.'

'We've got our very own scoop,' says Ralph thoughtfully. 'Can we print this Rupert?'

'No, Ralph. We can't. The most we could print is that an unnamed man is helping police with their enquiries. Innocent until proven guilty. Lev is a work colleague you know, we shouldn't be so quick to condemn him.' Bless him, Rupert is so honourable.

'No, no, of course not.' Ralph seems disappointed. 'Christ,' he goes on, 'that WPC was a big piece wasn't she. Wouldn't want to meet her down a dark alley.'

Lucy and I exchange glances and shake our heads in unison.

Chapter Ten

Dad's been in hospital for over three weeks now and he doesn't seem to be improving at all, in fact he's worse, lost in another world. He's had a barrage of tests and, yet they still can't find anything physically wrong with him.

A conversation that I had with Sister Kathy comes back to me now. Dad had only been in there for a few days and I asked her what she thought was wrong with him and she told me that it was best to wait and see. As usual I never know when to let it drop so I pressed her, and she reluctantly said she thought he had dementia.

Shocked, I said that it couldn't be because everyone knows that dementia takes years to show and Dad had become ill so quickly. She gave a sad smile and said she's seen it many times and it can be really quick. I refused to believe her then, but now I'm having my doubts.

Dad's settled in and is happy in his own way even if he doesn't have a clue where he is. Every visit he tells me that he's been talking to Mum on the radio and she's really looking forward to visiting. Nick is shocked at his deterioration when he visits as he usually only manages to see him at the weekend, but because I see him every other day, it's not so noticeable to me.

It's a slow Friday afternoon at work and the heat wave is back; we have all the windows open but there's no breeze, just the sounds from the precinct. Time is dragging and I'm not helping myself by constantly looking at the clock. The desk fan is directing a lovely cool breeze at me which is okay as long as I don't move from my desk. I had to fight Ian for it when I found it in the stationery cupboard and the only reason he hasn't pinched it is because I told him if he did I'd cut the plug off. The downside is that everything on my desk must be weighted down to stop it blowing away.

I look at my watch; three o'clock, two more hours to go.

I get up and wander into the tea room and draw myself a glass of water. The sink is filthy, and someone's obviously had spaghetti hoops recently as the plughole is full of them. I will not clean the sink. Again. I must be the only person who ever does it.

I close the door and sit at the table and use the opportunity to ring Nick.

He picks up straight away and I hear voices and music, the chinking of glasses, sounds of a bar.

'Hey, Sis, how's it hanging.'

'Yeah, good. How about you?'

'In Soho, doing a shoot in Barney's Bar for Solo menswear.'

'Sounds like you're on a night out.'

'I wish,' he lowers his voice. 'Bitch of a fashion editor, no-one can do anything right. I'd like to knock his goofy teeth right down his fucking throat.'

I laugh. 'Just think of the pay packet.'

'Believe me that's the only thing that's keeping me here. Sorry about the weekend, I'd much rather be there than here. Don't know why we have to shoot on a Saturday and Sunday. Loads of punters watching us too. Stupid idea.'

We must do something about paying Dad's bills as we don't know how long he's going to be in hospital. So, I'm going to Dad's tomorrow morning to look for the Power of Attorney. Nick remembers Dad getting us to sign it just after Mum died so fingers crossed I'll be able to find it.

'It's fine, don't worry. I'm sure it'll be in his desk, you know what a tidy freak Dad is. If I can't find it, you can help me look for it next weekend.'

'How is the old fella?'

'Happy enough but away with the fairies. He hasn't even asked about the house or going home. He still thinks he's in a hotel and Mum's coming to visit.'

Nick laughs. 'At least he's happy, it could be so much worse.'

He's right of course. We've seen some of the other patients and while a few of them are like Dad, some of them are pitiful. One lady lies in bed crying 'help me' the whole time, over and over again. I dread to think what sort of hell she's trapped in. Another old man shuffles around the room constantly, stopping to pick up imaginary objects from the floor. So yes, Dad is lucky. He's living a nice dream, not a nightmare like some other poor souls.

We chat for a while longer and then I reluctantly hang up as I've been away from my desk for too long. Just hope my fan is still there when I get back.

The fan's still there and so is Bert who's leaning on my desk gasping for breath, a screwed-up invoice clutched in his hand.

I extract the invoice from his grip. 'Thanks. Do

you want to sit down, Bert?' I pull out my chair for him and he flops into it and draws a shuddering breath.

'Can I get you anything Bert? Glass of water?' Or maybe an oxygen tank or defibrillator.

'No, sokay,' he gasps, thumping his chest. 'Be alright in a minute.'

'You want to put your foot down and tell Lev to bring his own invoices up,' calls Ian from across the room. 'Taking a bloody liberty sending a man of your age up and down those stairs.'

The police released Lev without charge after a few hours. His wife Dagmar had turned him in to the police as she thought he'd been having an affair and wanted revenge. She was the one who scratched his face, but Lev let himself be arrested rather than admit that a woman had done it. Dagmar's been charged with wasting police time, but Lev has forgiven her.

'It's fine.' Bert gasps, flapping his hand at Ian.

Ralph comes out of his office for his daily three o'clock mooch. He claps Bert on the back.

'You all right mate? You're not going to peg out or anything are you?'

Bert flaps his hand again, his breathing slowly returning to normal.

'Good, cos I don't fancy giving you the kiss of life if you get my drift. Now, when you get back downstairs you tell Lev to get his skinny arse up here because I want a word with him.'

Lev hasn't been in the office since he was arrested, too embarrassed. It's probably just as well as we're all feeling slightly uncomfortable that we were so ready to believe he was a murderer.

The killer is still at large, and Glenda is still

missing. No-one's coming out and saying it but there's not much hope of her being found alive. The post mortem results on Suzanne Jenkins have come back and it looks as if she was killed within a day of going missing. Strangled. The story even made the nationals for a while, some bright spark at the Sun called the murderer *The Frogham Throttler* and it seems to have stuck. It was hot news for a while but the lack of an arrest over the last few weeks has seen the broadcast vans in the precinct disappear one by one. No more blondes doing their piece to camera in front of the supermarket. We did wonder if they'd be back when Lev was arrested but as the police only held him for a few hours it never made the news.

Bert eventually recovers enough to clomp down the stairs and shortly afterwards we hear Lev's hesitant footsteps, then silence. He's lurking on the landing.

'Come in Lev, I know you're out there,' shouts Ralph.

Lev slinks into the office, head down, looking at the floor.

'Right Lev, time to put a stop to this hiding downstairs. You've done nothing wrong so there's no need to be embarrassed.'

Lev peers out from under his baseball cap. He doesn't look happy.

'You think I throttler.'

'No, no, course we don't Lev, we never thought that did we?'

Lucy keeps her head down and Ian smirks.

'Of course, we didn't think that Lev,' says Rupert, 'That was the furthest thing from our minds.'

I murmur agreement, Lucy nods and Ian just grins.

Lev looks around at us, his face pinched and sad. 'Why no one defend me? You all see that she-devil arrest me and no one speak.'

'Now come on Lev, no-one believed you were guilty, but we can hardly argue with the police, can we?'

Lev doesn't look convinced. Ralph's patience now exhausted, he puts his arm around Lev's shoulders in a brotherly fashion.

'That's enough of that now Lev, because quite frankly you're starting to give my arse a headache. So, no more sending Bert up here. You don't want his death on your conscience now do you?' Not the best choice of words.

Lev looks slightly mollified, mutters his agreement and plods back down the stairs.

'Was it my imagination or did he have a black eye?' asks Ian when he's gone.

'Surely not,' says Rupert.

'He did. Expect his wife's been knocking him around again, or,' Ian adds, 'he really is the throttler and he's done another one.'

I'm buzzed into Blossom Unit and the smell of shepherd's pie and cabbage tells me what's been for dinner. Dad's settled on the sofa in the television room watching the news.

'Oh, hello.' He looks round at me and smiles.

'Hello, Dad.' I bend to kiss him. 'How are you?'

'Not so bad.' He carries on watching the news then turns to me when it's finished.

'There's been a right to-do here today.'

'Has there?'

'You know that lady that does the knitting? The

138

one that's always sat out there?' He nods in the direction of the lounge.

I look through the internal window to the lounge.

'There's no point in looking, she's not there,' he says, 'she's dead.'

'Dead?' I'm shocked, she looked fine the other day.

'Very sudden it was, lots of rushing around and important looking people up here. There was even a copper came in earlier, they have to have one for an unexplained death. Apparently, they found her dead in her bed this morning.'

'God, that's awful, poor woman.'

'It is,' Dad says thoughtfully. 'She'll never finish that scarf now. That's why I'm in here, watching the news. I thought it might have been on by now, but it hasn't.'

'Hellooo.' Liz the co-ordinator is hovering in the doorway. 'Mind if I join you? I can tell you what Dad's been doing today.' I swiftly get up and practically haul Dad out of his chair.

'Oh, what a shame we're just going, perhaps another time.' Never if I can help it. I propel a confused Dad towards the door. He's my Dad not yours. Mr Russell to you, Liz. She blocks the doorway with her body and I stand in front of her until she takes the hint and moves ever so slightly aside. She gives me a look of pure venom as I squeeze past her with Dad.

The corridor to Dad's room has four doors leading from it, Dad's is number four. The first two rooms' inhabitants are tucked up in bed fast asleep and the third room's occupant is sitting in her chair knitting. The knitting lady.

I turn to Dad and raise my eyebrows.

'Well,' he says, 'she doesn't know she's dead yet.'

The window in Dad's room looks out onto an enclosed courtyard. It's not a very exciting view, a spindly looking tree next to a scrubby patch of grass which looks as if it's just been cut. It's absolutely stifling in here, I open the window to let some air in and the smell of freshly mown grass drifts in on warm air.

Dad settles himself in the armchair which is the only chair in the room and I sit on the bed.

'Look at them two.' dad laughs, nodding at the window. 'They're non-stop you know, lugging those cases around all day, they must be fit as fiddles. Never known a hotel so busy.'

I agree with him and we sit and watch the invisible porters for a while then Dad picks the newspaper up and we begin the hunt for his glasses.

I open each drawer in his chest of drawers one by one but can't find them. Wardrobe next, but first I check the bin.

'Hey you! Get out of my room!' A white-haired lady is standing in the doorway pointing at me. She's tiny, probably not even five foot. She has a sweet little doll-like face, but her expression is one of indignant rage.

'YOU! Get out! This is my room. You can't just go through my things.'

She stomps towards me and doesn't look happy. Dad looks over.

'Oh hello,' he says obliviously. 'I don't think we've met.' He gets out of the chair and puts his hand out to her. 'I'm Tom.'

She looks at him with something like hatred then raises her hand and I think she's going to hit him when a man's voice stops her.

'MUM! It's not your room, come out!'

Her hand stops in mid-air and she looks at Dad and then at me uncertainly.

'Mother! Come on, I'll take you to your room.' The speaker comes into the room and we both look at each other in surprise.

It's Detective Inspector Peters.

He bends down and puts his arm around her. 'Come on Mum, you're getting confused. Let's go back to your room.' He guides her away but she's not convinced, looking back over her shoulder at me and Dad accusingly.

'She seems very nice,' says Dad.

I stir my coffee and Detective Inspector Peters does the same, adding another packet of sugar to his. We're sitting on uncomfortable plastic chairs around a corner table in the hospital cafeteria. When I came out of Blossom Unit after visiting Dad the Detective Inspector was outside. I was shocked when I realised he was waiting for me, and even more so when he suggested we go for a coffee.

So, here we are.

'Fancy meeting you in a place like this Detective Inspector,' I say in an attempt to break the ice.

'Gareth, please. I'm not on duty now.'

'Gareth,' I repeat. 'How long has your mother been here? I haven't seen you here before.'

'Two days this time. This is the third time she's been in, she's probably spent eight months out of the last two years in here. They'll stabilise her, sort her medication out and she'll go back to the home. Your Dad?'

'Just over three weeks. They're still trying to find out what's wrong with him.'

He nods. 'Mum was in here three months before they diagnosed her. Dementia.'

'Does your mother know who you are?' I blurt out, then think how rude I sound, but he doesn't seem bothered.

'Sometimes. Sometimes she thinks I'm her Dad. I think she knows I'm family but it's all mixed up. I don't put her right, there's no point, she's lost the capacity to understand. She gets very confused, as you saw.'

I drink my coffee and wonder why we're here and I can't think of a damn thing to say.

'Do you think Glenda's still alive?' I think I need to tape my mouth up.

He smiles. 'You know I can't talk about that.'

'Do you remember,' he goes on, 'the first time we met?'

'Yes of course, when you came into the office about the telephone call.'

'You're not a very good liar, Louise.' He looks at me and smiles, it seems I'm not going to be let off the hook this time.

'No, I'm not. I'm a crap liar and of course I remember the first time we met although for obvious reasons I'd rather forget.' I bang my cup down with a clang. An elderly couple a few tables away look round with pursed lips of disapproval. 'So yes, I remember that I was a drunken mess and I made an exhibition of myself and I was lucky not be charged. So what's your point?'

He laughs. He actually laughs. I pick up my handbag and get up to leave.

'No, no, don't go, please don't go, sit down, sit down.' He's trying not to laugh now.

I sit down and cross my arms. The elderly couple are frowning and whispering to each other now. I resist the urge to poke my tongue out at them.

'Look, I'm sorry, I didn't mean to laugh at you or embarrass you. When you came in that night it'd been a pretty dull shift at the station and you brightened my evening.'

'I'd rather forget that night, I made a complete fool of myself and I cringe just thinking about it.'

'Don't be so hard on yourself, you sobered up pretty quickly.'

I stare at the table.

'And you were a model prisoner.' I sneak a look from under my eyelashes; he's laughing again.

'I'm glad you think it's so funny.'

'Well it was. Threatening behaviour with a mop wasn't it?' His eyes are really twinkly. Hadn't noticed that before.

'Might have been,' I say mulishly.

'And you made a very glamorous prisoner.'

Despite myself I smile. Always a sucker for a compliment. Is he flirting with me?

'Is it just you and your Dad or do you have any other family?' Is he fishing to find out if I'm single?

'Just a brother but he can't come very often as he lives away. How about you?'

'No. Just me. Only child. Married to the job.'

So, we're both single. A sudden feeling of something like happiness bubbles to the surface.

'So,' he goes on, 'are you doing anything tomorrow

night?'

Direct, I like it.

'No, I'm not doing anything tomorrow night.'

'How does a meal sound? I mean, would you like to come out with me tomorrow evening?'

I make him wait a while before I answer, a little bit of revenge. He starts to look uncomfortable, so I put him out of his misery. Also, I don't want him to change his mind.

'Yes, I'd love to.'

As soon as I'm inside Dad's house I go around all the rooms and open the windows. The place smells fusty where it's been closed up. It's only half past ten but the day is already heating up.

Everything looks the same, but it doesn't feel like the same. Dad's presence made it a home; now it's just a house. I wonder if Dad will ever be able to come back here.

I give myself a mental slap, no moping, get on with it. First place to look: Dad's desk.

Mahogany, with two drawers on each side and a worktop that is twice the size of my desk at work. It's been in the study for as long as I can remember, Mum used to let Nick and I play schools on it when Dad was at work. After two hours I'm still looking; it's my own fault, I keep finding stuff that I want to look at. Not that I'm in a hurry, I have all day.

And a date with the Detective Inspector tonight. Must stop calling him that.

There's one whole drawer full of birthday cards to Dad and Mum from Nick and I, years old, dating back to when we were little. They've kept all of them and I've been through every single one. I've found an old chocolate box with pink roses on the front which is full of photographs of Mum and Dad when they first met, and I can't stop looking at them. They look so young, another lifetime when Nick and I weren't even thought of.

I finally find the Power of Attorney at the bottom of the last drawer I look in, inside an envelope marked 'Power of Attorney'. Typical Dad, bless him. So neat, tidy and organised. I pull it out of the envelope and read it; I signed it but have absolutely no memory of doing so. Looking at the date it was quite soon after Mum died so Dad was obviously putting everything in order in case anything happened to him.

The rest of the drawer is mainly full of bank statements and old cheque books. I put the Power of Attorney on the desk and push the drawer back in.

The drawer sticks, and I can't get it to go back in, something is stopping it, maybe something has fallen down the back. I give the drawer a sharp yank and the whole drawer comes flying out and lands with a thwack on the floor. God I'm so clumsy. I pick it up and try to line it up to get it back in when I see something flapping on the underside of the drawer. I turn the drawer over and there's a brown envelope taped to the bottom. The tape is brown with age and the envelope is half hanging off which is probably why the drawer got stuck.

Intrigued, I pull the envelope and it comes away easily. I open it and inside there's a sheet of paper. I unfold it and am immediately disappointed, it's just a death certificate.

I smooth it out on the desk and read it. I read it again. I actually rub my eyes in disbelief and read it again. Everything is right; the name, the date of birth. Except for the bit that's wrong. Very wrong.

I'm looking at my own death certificate.

Chapter Eleven

I try on three different outfits before I decide on a pale blue linen dress with a pair of strappy wedges.

I look out of the window; no sign of him yet. My date.

When I left Dad's house I'd decided to cancel tonight as I couldn't even think straight. But once I'd been home a couple of hours I changed my mind. I don't think I could stand my own company this evening with the same thoughts going round and round in my head on a loop.

So. Here we are. I look out of the window again and Gareth is just climbing out of a black open top sports car. I gawp for a moment, I didn't expect him to turn up in a police car, but a sports car? He looks straight at me as he walks up the path and I hurriedly move away from the blinds.

Great. So now I look like a desperate spinster waiting for her date to turn up. He does look gorgeous though; he's wearing a soft blue shirt with cream chinos. Doesn't look like a copper at all.

'Hi!' I open the front door with a bright smile on my face. 'I thought I heard a car.' I hear the clicking of Sprocket's claws on the kitchen floor as he hears me open the front door.

'Hi yourself.' I feel Gareth's appraising gaze on me and I'm pleased that I've made an effort to look nice.

Sprocket stands statue-like in the kitchen doorway. He stares at Gareth without blinking.

'Hello fella.'

Sprocket stares at Gareth for a few more moments then waddles over to him, tail wagging slowly.

Gareth kneels and rubs Sprocket's ears; his tail wags faster and he gazes up at Gareth adoringly.

Well. He's passed the first test.

'Right Sprocket. In the kitchen. You know the drill.'

Sprocket ignores me, and I have to drag him away to shut him in the kitchen so we can leave. I close the front door to the sound of him howling.

'I take it he doesn't like being left on his own?'

'He's fine normally. Just showing off. He'll stop as soon as we're gone.' Hopefully. I can still hear him when we get to the car.

Gareth opens the passenger door for me and I slide onto the plump red leather seat.

He walks round and gets in and starts the engine.

'Up or down?'

'Sorry?'

'Roof. Up or down? I can put it up if you'd rather.'

'Down is fine,' I say confidently, as if I've been sitting in convertibles all my life. I've never been in one before, this is going to be fun. It's a lovely warm evening and I can't wait to feel the breeze in my hair and the evening sun on my face.

'Thought we'd go to a nice little gastro pub I know. Just outside Frogham near Puckleberry village, should be there in about twenty minutes. It's called The Gamekeeper, have you been there before?'

'No, I haven't.'

It's really quaint, oak beams and good food. I think

you'll like it.'

'Sounds great.' I settle back into the seat.

'You look lovely by the way.' He fixes his twinkly eyes on me.

'Thank you.' The engine roars into life and we zoom off.

We arrive at The Gamekeeper and pull onto the rough ground that serves as a car park behind it. It's a typical country pub, painted white with black cross beams and a shabby thatched roof.

On reflection the decision of *roof down* may have been a mistake. The warm breeze I was expecting was more of a stiff wind and my eyes are stinging a bit as well. I don't suppose Gareth thought I looked very lovely with my hands clamped over my head trying to stop my hair from flying everywhere and my eyes squinting and watering from the wind.

Gareth gets out of the car then comes round and holds the door open for me like a proper gentleman. I haul myself inelegantly out of the car as all my joints also seem to have seized up. He looks as pristine as when he picked me up.

We both duck as we go into the pub through the low back door. Obviously designed for short people. The room is low and dark in the way of old pubs and I follow Gareth to the bar.

'What would you like?'

'White wine, please.'

He orders the drinks and I use the opportunity to excuse myself, so I can tidy my hair up.

I squeeze myself into the tiny toilet at the back of the restaurant and can't believe what I see in the rust speckled mirror. Or maybe I can, I should probably just have stayed home. My freshly washed and blow-dried hair, which before we left fell in soft waves around my shoulders, now resembles a greasy mop. The combination of the warm wind and my desperate attempts to keep it from flying everywhere have pulled every bit of wave out of it and it hangs limply around my head.

The crisp linen dress that I was so pleased with is now like a crumpled tea towel. The leather seat and my sweaty legs have pretty much ruined it.

To finish it off the wind has made my eyes water and my mascara has run down my face. To say I feel a mess would be an understatement.

I rummage in my handbag and find a comb and attempt to drag it through my hair. No luck. The only way those tangles will be coming out is when I wash it. I wet a paper towel and dab at the mascara on my face. I dab as much of the mascara off as I can along with most of my foundation.

I spend so long faffing around in there that Gareth is probably on dessert by now.

I emerge from the fluorescent glare of the toilets into the gloom of the pub and it takes a moment for me to see Gareth. He's seated at a table in the corner of the bar by the fire. I start to walk over and am nearly there when I stumble on the ancient flagstone floor. I completely lose my footing and can't stop myself. The floor rushes up to meet me when a pair of strong arms catch me just before I smash my head into the floor.

'Steady on!'

I gaze up into those twinkly eyes. Could this evening possibly get any worse?

'You okay?'

'Yes. I'm fine.' I step away from him and sit down. 'Thank you for catching me.' Great. Now I sound like a complete idiot.

'Lucky I've still got the rugby reflexes,' he says, sitting down. He grins.

'Well I'm glad you find it so funny. Have a good laugh at my hair at the same time. You could have warned me what the wind would do.'

'What's wrong with your hair? It looks fine to me.'

'Really?' I'm incredulous, 'REALLY?' I almost shout at him. 'Look at me, I'm a mess.' I feel like crying.

He reaches over and puts his hand over mine.

'Hey, I'm sorry. I wasn't laughing at you.'

'No. I'm sorry. I shouldn't have come.' I should have stayed at home. I am dead after all.

He looks crestfallen and I realise what I've said.

'I've had a rotten day – stuff to do with my Dad, so maybe I shouldn't have inflicted myself on you. I didn't mean I didn't want to come.'

'Well, in that case,' he says picking up a menu, 'let's order some food and start over.' Those twinkly eyes again.

'Okay, let's.'

'And just for the record,' he says, 'you look gorgeous, wild hair or not.'

'Up or down?'

'I don't think it'll make any difference now, so down.' I smile. 'It's a beautiful evening, be a shame to shut it out.' Warm, and still. The sort of stillness that you only get in the countryside.

'Down it is.' He grins, 'I like that dishevelled look anyway.'

We pull out of the car park, the tyres crunching over the gravel. I don't bother trying to hold my hair down and my eyes don't stream this time.

I've had such a lovely evening. Gareth is so funny and easy to talk to; the evening flew by and we were the only people left when we realised that the staff were waiting for us to leave. We'd hardly got out of the door when we heard the bolts and locks being shot across. We both collapsed in giggles and couldn't stop, I don't know why it was so funny, it just was.

It seems much quicker getting home than it did going, and we pull up outside my house.

Gareth kills the engine and turns to me.

'Thank you, I really enjoyed tonight.'

'Me too,' I say.

We lean slowly towards each other, neither of us willing to make the first move.

'So,' I say, 'would you like to come in for a coffee? I'm sure Sprocket would love to see you.'

'Coffee would be good. And of course, I wouldn't want to disappoint Sprocket.'

Neither of us makes a move to get out and the break the spell. We inch closer.

The opening bars of Depeche Mode shatter the silence between us and we jump apart.

Your own personal Jesus, someone to hear your prayers...

'Christ, sorry, I'll have to get this.' Gareth pulls his mobile out of his pocket. He moves over in his seat away from me and puts the phone to his ear.

I sit back trying not to listen but still hear Gareth say 'yes' and 'no' and 'when' several times.

He finishes the call and turns to me.

'I'm really sorry but I have to go. Duty calls.'

'It's okay.' I shrug. 'another time.'

'No really,' he says. 'I am sorry. I'd like nothing better than to come in for a coffee.' He grins. 'To see Sprocket of course.'

'He'll be really disappointed.'

'Not as disappointed as me,' he says then leans over and kisses me gently on the lips, 'Goodnight Louise, see you soon?'

'Reach out touch faith,' I say with a smile.

'A fellow fan?' He seems delighted.

'Can't beat a bit of Depeche Mode. I have every album.' I laugh.

'Me too.' He kisses me again. 'I knew you were perfect,' he says, pulling me closer. I rest my head on his shoulder and we sit in stillness for a moment.

I close my eyes and enjoy the closeness of him, I could sit here all night.

'Louise?'

'Yes?' I say dreamily.

'I'm sorry, I have to go.'

I sit up. 'Of course you do.' I pick my handbag up from the footwell and clamber out of the car.

'Goodnight.'

'Night, Gareth.'

He watches from the car as I unlock the front door and go in, I give him a wave and he zooms off down the road.

I float into the kitchen and wrap my arms around Sprocket and give him a big cuddle, his cold nose pressed into my neck.

'I've had a lovely evening Sprocket, with a really nice man.'

Sprocket sighs and I stroke his ears feeling all warm and fuzzy. The warm fuzzy feeling lasts precisely five minutes before the fact of my death comes crashing down on me. Oh well, it was good while it lasted. Somehow, I've managed not to think about it all night, every time it threatened to start dragging me down I batted it away like a tennis ball. But now I don't have Gareth to distract me I think it'll be a different story.

I get ready for bed and clean my teeth, but I know that I won't sleep; not with the thing that I'm trying not to think about buzzing around in my head. I decide it's pointless trying so go back downstairs and find a notebook and pen and settle on the sofa with Sprocket on my feet. All the self-help gurus say that if you write down the problem it'll help you solve it. So, I head up the page:

Facts:

I have a birth certificate in my name.

I have a death certificate in my name which states I died at three months old, a cot death.

Reasons for finding a death certificate in my name:

1. I have a twin
2. It's a fake certificate, someone's idea of a joke
3. I'm not who I think I am, I'm someone else
   3.1 If I'm someone else what about Mum, Dad and Nick?
4. I'm dead. I'm a ghost.

I sit and chew the end of the pen but as hard as I try I just can't think of any other reasons. I cross out number four as I'm obviously not a ghost.

Okay, number one, I have a twin sister – this is possible. But why would she have the same name as me? Perhaps Mum and Dad preferred her to me so changed my name to hers. Pretty farfetched and unlikely, but possible.

Number two – the certificate's a fake. I grab my laptop, open it up and Google it and am amazed at how easy it is to get a fake death certificate. There are hundreds of websites advertising how to obtain your own fake death certificate. Apparently, it's a hilarious joke to play on someone, but more likely just their way of selling fake ID legally.

But I can't imagine Mum or Dad thinking this would be remotely funny and, also the envelope and certificate look pretty old.

Number three – I'm not who I think I am.

If I'm not who I think I am, then who am I? This is the most likely and also the scariest. Because if I'm not Louise Russell then I'm someone else who's been brought up as Louise Russell.

Number three point one – Are Mum, Dad and Nick someone else too? Is Dad really a spy and we're all foreign sleeper agents who have taken dead people's identities? Is that why he's obsessed with M15? I know this is farfetched and in the realms of fantasy but isn't finding your own death certificate farfetched?

If we're all sleeper agents where are their death certificates? Why is there only mine? Or I am the only one that doesn't know and they have their own death certificates? Do Dad and Nick (and Mum) know they're sleeper agents but haven't told me because they think I couldn't handle it?

Also, finding a family where everyone has died would be a bit too convenient for foreign spies, so I think I'll dismiss this one too.

Which leaves me with not being who I thought I was. It also leaves the one explanation which I've been trying not to think about but seems most obvious.

What if the real Louise Russell died and I was stolen as a replacement?

First things first – I need to make sure the death certificate is genuine.

There's no time like the present. I search for family tree websites. There are loads. Before I have too much time to think about it and put myself off of the idea I sign up for a free fourteen-day trial on *Family Search*.

I decide to start with Mum; I type in Betty Croker and her date of birth and sit back and wait.

74 records found

I was expecting a lot as Mum's maiden name is quite common. Lucky we're not called Smith, I suppose. I scroll through and there she is; so she definitely existed. I do the same for Dad, then Nick, and up they pop. So far, so good. I put my own name and date of birth in and there I am.

Next, I put Mum's details in to see if there's a death registered in her name. There is.

Next, I put in Dad's, then Nick's. No match.

Okay. Deep breath. I put my own name and date of death in and wait, watching the whirly thing chugging away.

It's a match. There is it in black and white.

So if Louise Russell is dead, who am I?

Although I have a death certificate in my name I have also carried on living. Is this possible? Wouldn't I have flagged up as dead when I got married or applied for a passport?

I know the answer to this: I wouldn't.

One of my temping jobs was in a pensions department of a large company. One of the pensioners died but no-one notified us, and her husband continued to draw her pension for twenty years. He was only found out when he moved house and didn't notify the company. His pay slip was returned to the office and the tracing agency used to trace his wife's new address discovered she died twenty years previously and voila! The game was up. If he'd written in with his new address as he'd done several times before he'd still be drawing the pension now.

I think back to my childhood. Did I feel different?

No. I didn't.

I pull out one of the photograph albums that I brought home from Dad's and flick through it.

Nick looks like Dad – everyone agrees about this, he is a younger version of Dad only a better looking one. I look like Mum, everyone agrees about this too. I've always trotted this out myself, 'Oh Nick looks just like Dad and I take after Mum.' I've never questioned this, although I could never see it myself, but I couldn't see the resemblance between Dad and Nick. I can never really see family resemblances, probably because of the age difference.

I look at a picture of Mum and Dad on their silver wedding anniversary. They were probably around the age that Nick and I are now, and I can see that Nick does look a lot like Dad. The same direct smile, even the same hair. I'd never realised how handsome Dad was, he was just Dad to me. I don't look anything like him, or Nick.

I look at the picture of Mum. I try to be objective and compare a selfie on my phone with her. We have the same wavy fair hair and we're the same height, but if I look at individual features we're not alike at all.

To someone who knows we're related it's easy to say we look alike but actually, we don't.

I am the cuckoo in the nest.

I suddenly feel very alone. Nothing has changed as far as everyone else is concerned but everything has changed for me. I wish I could talk to someone about it, but who? How can I talk to Nick? I don't want him to feel like I do or even worse. What if he already knows? I can't believe he does; he's useless at keeping secrets. He admits it himself; 'don't tell me any secrets,' he says, 'you know I can't keep my gob shut.'

But the big issue is how would they get away with substituting me for a dead baby? People would know I was dead. I pull out my death certificate and look at it again; the address is London, so it was before we moved to Frogham. Mum and Dad always told the story of how Dad got his job in Hendersons and we moved to Frogham when I was a baby. Now I come to think of it they never exactly said how old I was when we moved, and I never asked, it didn't seem important.

They had no other family, no brothers or sisters, so they just left their life in London and started a completely new life here.

Perhaps that's a lie too. Maybe I do have aunts and uncles, but they had to be deleted from their lives because they would have known I was dead.

My eyes feel gritty and my shoulders are aching from hunching over the laptop. I look at the clock and it's nearly a quarter to three. I need to go to bed, I move my feet and wake a snoring Sprocket who is not impressed. I drag myself up the stairs and collapse into bed. I'm so tired, I could sleep for a week.

I wake with a start.

The room is dark, and I can't see the clock so have no idea what time it is. The dream woke me; I was dreaming about blood. I can't remember the detail; it's already fading, but I know what the dream refers to. A memory has come back to me that meant nothing at the time but now makes me wonder.

I was eighteen and working as a junior clerk in Jacksons, a large insurance company. The blood transfusion service was touting for people to give blood and Jacksons had given a room over to them for the day and were giving people the opportunity to give blood during work time. Of course, because it was a bit of time off with a free cup of tea and a biscuit everyone did it. It was surprising how many big beefy men came over all peculiar at the sight of their own blood.

When I got home from work I was ridiculously pleased with myself and started to tell Mum all about it. She was mashing potatoes while I laid the table for dinner and she reacted in an odd way. She got quite agitated and told me I shouldn't have done it; I was too young and what were they doing encouraging youngsters to give blood when they were still growing. She wouldn't shut up about it until I promised her that I wouldn't give anymore.

At the time I thought it was just her being over protective again but was there more to it than that? I never received my blood donor card through the post and now I wonder if Mum made sure I never got it. Was she afraid I'd somehow discover that she wasn't my mother? To live with a lie all your life – were Mum and Dad capable of that? I can't believe they were.

I snuggle back down in bed and wake for sleep to take me.

I'm going to visit Dad tomorrow.

And I'm going to ask him who I really am.

Chapter Twelve

'I want to go home. Can you take me home?' Dad has his coat on, a bulging holdall in his hand.

Sister Kathy is hovering behind him trying to catch my eye. She made a beeline for me as soon as I was buzzed in, but Dad beat her to it.

I look at her, I look at Dad, uncertain what to do.

'Louise! I tried to ring you, but you wouldn't answer. I'm ready to go home NOW.'

'There's paperwork to complete Tom so why don't you have a nice cup of tea first?' Sister Kathy puts her hand on Dad's arm, but he shakes it off impatiently.

'I don't want a cup of tea. I WANT to go home. My mother's waiting for me.'

'Well I'm afraid there are formalities, so you'll have to be patient.'

Dad hesitates so I grab him by the arm and steer him round to the lounge.

'Come on Dad, I could do with a drink before we go.' He doesn't quite dig his heels into the carpet, but he resists all the way there and it's like pushing a statue.

The sofa is free so before he can argue I yank his coat and holdall off him and push him down into the seat. I sit down next to him.

'So, Dad, what's been happening? Why the rush to go home?'

'I need to get home, my mother's waiting.'

'She won't mind if you're a few minutes late.'

He shakes his head, bewildered.

'There's reason I need to be there, but I can't remember what it is.'

'That's okay. I forget things all the time.'

'You're humouring me.' He stares straight at me, the old Dad back for a moment. 'I can't remember. I wish I could remember, it's all mixed up.'

'Perhaps I can help you remember.' I mouth 'thanks' as Kathy puts two teas on the table. 'Do you want me to try and help you?'

He shrugs.

'Okay, do you know where you are?'

'I'm in hotel, I think. I'm not completely sure. Betty's coming but she's taking so long to get here. I think maybe they won't let her go.' He looks near to tears.

'Who won't let her go Dad?'

He's silent for a moment, a frown on his face as he tries to remember. 'I don't know!' he almost wails, 'But I know I should have looked after her better, took better care of her.' He gulps. 'It's all my fault. Everything's my fault.'

I put my hand on his shoulder. 'What's your fault, Dad?'

'She wasn't well you know, wasn't her fault. She was only trying to help. I shouldn't have gone to work, should have stayed at home with her.' Dad puts his head in his hands. 'And it was too late, I left it too late. We could have made it right, but it was too late.' He takes a juddering breath then starts to cry in great choking sobs. I can't bear it, I've never seen him like this before.

I throw my arms around him and hold him tight. Over his shoulder Knitting Lady is watching from her armchair, needles suspended mid-knit. She looks very well for someone who's dead.

The sobs gradually get quieter and then he pushes my arms away and looks at me.

'Who are you? Where's my daughter? Where's Louise?'

'I'm your daughter, Dad. I'm Louise.'

'No you're not.' He gets up out of the chair and stands in front of me, studying my face.

'I don't know who you are, but you're not Louise.'

I've heard Dad say this many times now, but it still hurts.

He picks his coat up and puts it on and carefully buttons it up. 'My daughter's coming to get me, *she's* taking me home.' He picks up the holdall. 'And if you don't mind me saying I think you've got a cheek pretending to be someone you're not. I'm not stupid you know.'

He straightens his shoulders and puts his head up and walks over to Kathy. He talks to her and points at me and shakes his head. I can't hear what she says but it seems to placate him, and he trundles off in the direction of his room.

'We'll look after him my love.' Knitting Lady points at Dad with a needle. 'No need to worry about him, we'll take care of him.'

'Thank you.'

'I'm knitting him a scarf you know.' She holds up a greyish roll of knitting that looks as if it's been dragged around the floor. 'Nearly finished,' she says, clamping her tongue between her toothless gums. 'Just a few more rows.' She frowns as she

163

concentrates on putting one needle through a loop and the clack of the needles starts again.

I hear a noise behind me and look up to see Kathy settling herself in the chair Dad's just left.

'He's very confused.'

'He wants to go home,' I say flatly.

'They all want to go home,' she says. 'Although most of them can't remember where home is.'

'Can he come home?'

'No. He can't leave the unit. Maybe when we've found out what's wrong with him you could take him out for a few hours but for now it would do more harm than good.'

'He's a prisoner.'

'Well...'

'He is. He's a prisoner and may never go home and it's because of me. I should have left him alone in the home he loved. He was happy there. It's all my fault.'

'Listen.' Kathy puts her hand on my arm. 'Listen to me.'

Nothing she says is going to make me feel any better.

'You had no choice, he wasn't safe to be at home.'

'I could have looked after him, moved in with him.'

'You'd have to give up your job.'

'I could do that,' I say, 'my job's not that great.'

'Could you stay up all night, every night and watch him to make sure he doesn't wander out into the street? Watch him the whole time to make sure he doesn't harm himself? Climb out of the window? Fall down the stairs?'

I look at her.

'And that's now,' she says. 'If he gets worse what

164

then? He's not safe to be at home, he needs twenty-four-hour care with someone watching him the whole time. Why do you think we have cameras in the bedrooms? He's one of the lucky ones.' She smiles at my look of disbelief. 'Trust me, he is. He's got a family that love and care about him and want the best for him. Do you realise how many old people go through this on their own? Some poor souls have no one and by the time they get to us they've usually been picked up wandering the streets, terrified and alone. Or worse, they don't get to us because they've died, alone and afraid.'

'That's awful.'

'It is.' She pats my hand. 'So don't ever think that your Dad being in here is the worst thing that can happen because it could be so much worse. And I know it's horrible but at least he's had a good life, he's nearly eighty and he's been fit and healthy until now, so you have to be grateful for that.'

'He has, fit as a fiddle.'

'We had a gentleman in here last year, early onset dementia which progressed rapidly. He was fifty-one. He didn't recognise his wife or his teenage sons. Investment banker. Tragic. Dementia doesn't discriminate. I'm not belittling what's happening to your Dad, but it could be worse.'

She gets up from the chair. 'Anyway, you take care of yourself. I best get on.'

When she's gone I sit for a while pondering her words. She's right, it could be so much worse for Dad; I must keep telling myself that. I pick up my handbag and wander round to Dad's room.

Dad's put himself to bed and is fast asleep, his clothes are in a heap on the floor and he's put his pyjamas on. I stand over him and he looks so peaceful, as if he doesn't have a care in the world. I may as well go; so much for asking him who I really am, he's so confused there's not much point. I'll ask him next time. If he's not even worse.

Also you feel a bit relieved that you can leave now, pipes up a little voice in my head.

I say goodbye to Kathy on my way out and as I come out of the Blossom Unit doors I realise my phone's ringing. I pull it out of my handbag.

'Hi Louise, it's Gareth.'

'Hi.'

'Are you okay?'

No, I'm not. Definitely not. 'Yes, I'm fine. How are you?'

'I'm good thanks. Look, I've got bad news, but I wanted to tell you before you hear it anywhere else.'

'Oh.' I know what he's going to say. Can this day get any worse?

'Yes. Um. Okay. That call I took last night, it was about the case. They found another body.' He pauses, 'I'm really sorry but it's Glenda. A farmer found her in one of his fields last night when he was checking his sheep. Some attempt had been made to bury her, but it looks like a fox had started to dig her up.'

I think I'm going to be sick and I stand in the middle of the car park with my hand over my mouth. I must have made a retching sound as Gareth is gabbling in my ear.

'Shit. Sorry I shouldn't have told you that, you didn't need to know. I'm so, so sorry, I know she was your friend. I'm such an idiot.'

I take deep gulps of air and feel the colour return to my face. I wipe my eyes and my fingers come away wet. I didn't know I was crying. I don't know anything anymore.

'It's okay. It's not your fault. She wasn't even my friend, I only met her once. I didn't even like her for God's sake, but she shouldn't be dead. She didn't deserve to die.'

'She didn't, and we will get him. We're pulling out all the stops.'

I bet he says that all the time; it can't be easy, his job.

'Louise,' Gareth says, sounding concerned. 'I'm hoping to get away by seven, will you be in tonight? Shall I come round?'

He must be exhausted, he's been there since last night. The last thing he needs is to come round and put up with me when he really just wants to go home and sleep. It would be really selfish of me to take him up on his offer.

'Yes, I'll be in,' I say. 'Come over. I'll cook us something.'

I walk up the street with Sprocket bounding along beside me. I should go to Linda's and tell her about Glenda before she hears it on the news. I'll go after I've given Sprocket a walk. Delaying it, that's what I'm doing.

We reach the Rise and I see the familiar figures of Linda and Henry standing in the field, so I really can't put it off. Linda has her phone clamped to her ear, deep in conversation.

I walk up behind here and wait for her to finish. She doesn't realise I'm there until Henry barks at us and runs over.

'Oh! You made me jump. Didn't realise you were

there.' Her cheeks are flushed. 'I won't be a minute.' She turns her back to me and drops her voice, so I can't hear what she's saying apart from the odd giggle. Must be a man.

'Sorry about that.' She tucks her phone in her coat pocket.

'No need to be sorry, you didn't know I was there. You didn't need to hang up.'

'Oh, I was finished anyway.' She's definitely blushing now.

We amble along, past the fading police tape swinging in the breeze. I have to tell her about Glenda. I don't want to.

'So,' I say, 'who was it?'

'Who was who?' She seems flustered and a little worm of suspicion rears its head and waves at me.

'On the phone, who was it?'

'Oh, no one important.' She waves her hand. 'Just a friend.'

I nod. 'Friend got a name?'

'Oh, no one you know.' Her face is scarlet.

I stop, and she stops too, and I turn to face her. I look at her straight on, but she won't meet my eyes.

'It was Nick wasn't it?'

'Who?'

'Nick. As in. Nick. My brother.'

'Yes, it was.'

'So why lie?'

'I don't know. Just feel a bit awkward that's all. It's not like we've been on a date or anything. Just chatting.'

'For Christ's sake Linda, we're friends. If you want to go out with my brother that's fine – just don't expect too much from him, will you? You know he

168

doesn't do commitment.'

'Sorry.'

'Just promise me that if it all goes tits up you won't fall out with me. He's my brother and I love him dearly but he's a total shit when it comes to women.'

'Course I won't.' I can tell she doesn't believe me, like all the other women he gets tangled up with who think they can change him.

Linda smiles and links her arm through mine. 'So come on, tell me how the date went last night.'

'Hmm. Don't know that I will seeing as you're keeping secrets.' I laugh at her crestfallen face. 'No, it was great. He's lovely, funny and so easy to get on with. We went to a cute little pub out in the country, all beams and oak floors. Was lovely.'

Linda raises her eyebrows. 'You sound smitten, are you seeing him again? Did you invite him in for coffee?' She asks meaningfully.

'I did. But he never came in because he got a phone call and had to go to work, so that scuppered that. He's coming round tonight after work though. I said I'd cook for him.'

'Really?'

'Yeah, I know. Got a bit carried away, forgot I couldn't cook. Thought I'd do my signature dish of burnt fish fingers and beans.'

Linda laughs. 'You're not that bad.'

We both know I am.

'He must be keen, though, if he's coming round.'

Hope so. Now I must spoil everything and tell her about Glenda.

'So. The reason he got called away for work. . .'I let my voice trail off.

Linda looks at me and realisation dawns.

'They found a body in a field. It's Glenda.' I say it quickly to get it over with although I leave out the bit about the foxes.

She shakes her head and looks at the ground and we walk along in silence for a while.

'Poor Glenda. I can't believe it. Things like this don't happen in Frogham.'

They never used to, but they do now.

'Do they know how she died? How long she's been dead?'

'I don't know any details. It'll be on the news later, so I don't know whether they'll have more details by then.'

'It's just so awful. I just hope she didn't suffer.' She shudders, 'Poor, poor Glenda.'

We amble along in silence neither of us knowing what to say. There is nothing we can say that'll change the fact that Glenda's dead.

He could be here now, the Frogham Throttler. Might be marking one of us out as the next victim. I look around the field at the Sunday afternoon dog walkers and joggers. A youth with a man bun trots past and I look at him with suspicion. The sun goes behind a cloud for a moment and a shiver runs up my spine.

I turn to Linda. 'Shall we go back to yours? You can give me a fool proof recipe for tonight.'

'Good idea,' says Linda.

I think she's as eager as me to get home.

He could be watching us right now.

Oven on, lasagne in, timer set.

With Linda's written instructions I've cooked the mince, layered the pasta sheets and sauce, and sprinkled with cheese. It was quite easy really, don't know why I haven't done lasagne before. What can possibly go wrong?

I rip open the garlic bread packet which breaks into a thousand pieces and the bread catapults into the air. I just manage to catch it before it falls into Sprocket's waiting jaws.

I throw it into a baking tray. There, all done and ready. Sprocket is sitting looking at me in disappointment, he shuffles from foot to foot and a string of drool drops onto the floor.

'Not quick enough, Sprocket,' I tell him. Although if he had caught it I'd probably have wrestled him for it and served it up anyway. I check my watch; time for a quick change. I fly upstairs, quickly shower then put on a pair of pale green cropped chinos and a floaty white t-shirt. Pleased with what I see in the mirror I just get to the bottom of the stairs and the doorbell rings. He's early; must be keen.

I open the front door with a ready smile to see the Truth standing on my doorstep.

'Oh, hello, Norman.' How does he even know where I live?

'Hello, Louise.' He's holding a bunch of bedraggled flowers. 'I just wanted to say a proper thank you for finding Lulu.' He thrusts the flowers at me.

'Oh. Thank you. They're lovely but you really didn't need to, it was nothing really.'

'Sorry it's taken so long but I wasn't sure where you lived so I asked Linda and she told me.'

Thanks Linda.

He's hovering. I need to get rid of him.

'Well, thank you again for the flowers,' I say,

already closing the door. 'I'd invite you in, but I expect you're busy.'

'No. I'm not busy. Mother's at bingo tonight so it's my night off.' By the time he's finished speaking he's squeezed through the doorway into the hall and is in the lounge. I curse myself for inviting him in; although I didn't think I had. I'll never get rid of him now.

When Gareth arrives ten minutes later he finds Norman settled on my sofa with a mug of tea and Lulu nestled on his lap.

'This is Norman, he just popped in.'

'Hi Norman, nice to see you.'

'Hello Detective Inspector.' Norman shakes Gareth's hand. 'What a lovely surprise, didn't expect to see you here.'

Gareth settles down next to him on the sofa. 'Louise and I have known each other for years.' Norman says. Gareth looks meaningfully at the flowers lying on the coffee table.

'I'm just going to check on the lasagne and put these in water.' I pick the flowers up and go into the kitchen. I search the kitchen for a vase and can't find one. In desperation I cut the stems off the flowers and put them in an empty jam jar I've fished out of the recycling. They look awful, so I hide them behind the bread bin.

'So,' I say brightly as I walk back into the lounge, 'shouldn't be long now, another five minutes.' I look pointedly at Norman, mentally willing him to go. Sprocket is sitting on Gareth's lap looking very pleased with himself. I may as well go out and leave them to it.

'Smells delicious.' Norman sniffs the air. 'S'making

me feel very hungry. Have to fend for myself tonight. Mother's bingo night.' He nods at me. Cheeky sod.

Gareth raises his eyebrows and looks at me with a little smile.

'Yes, that certainly smells delicious,' Norman goes on. 'Lasagne you say? My absolute all-time favourite.'

I stand by the door twisting the tea towel around in my hands and Norman finally takes the hint and stands up.

'Come on Lulu old girl, there's a can of soup with my name on it at home.'

Oh, for God's sake. I sigh and give in to the inevitable.

'Would you like to stay for dinner Norman? There's plenty to go around.' Did I say that? It seems I did.

'Oh well, if you're sure...' He's already settling back down of the sofa. '...I'd love to.'

If Gareth is annoyed, he doesn't show it and I leave them chatting as I set the table and get the lasagne out of the oven. On the plus side the lasagne looks okay and may even be edible. I've managed to incinerate the garlic bread, but I don't have anymore, so I hack at it with the bread knife and fling it bad temperedly into a basket, hiding the blackened knobby ends at the bottom.

I put it all on the table and call Gareth and Norman.

'Thought we could have this with it.' Gareth hands me a bottle of red wine as he sits down. I hadn't even noticed he'd brought it with him.

'Oh, lovely, I'll get some glasses.' He gives me a lopsided smile and I see how tired he looks. He could probably do without me inviting random dog walkers in for dinner. I could too.

I put the glasses out while Gareth uncorks the wine.

'Not for me, thank you.' Norman holds his hand over the wine glass as if we're going to force him to drink. 'Have you got any orange squash? I've only got to smell wine and I go all peculiar.' He pulls a face. 'Makes me talk all sorts of nonsense.'

I go back out to the kitchen and rummage around and unearth a dusty bottle of lime juice cordial which is two years out of date. I open it and have a sniff; smells okay, drinks don't go off anyway. I pour a good glug of it into a pint glass and top it up out of the cold tap.

The lasagne's not bad actually; the garlic bread's pretty hard going but a mouthful of red wine mushes it up a bit and helps it go down. I zone out as Norman does most of the talking. I catch the odd 'God's honest truth' but I'm not really paying attention.

'Isn't that right Louise?'

'Sorry?'

'I was just telling Gareth how you saved Lulu's life.'

'I didn't save her life,' I say. 'I just happened to be in the right place at the right time.'

'She's being modest.' Norman points his fork at me. 'She went out of her way and I'll be forever grateful. I don't know what I'd have done if I hadn't got Lulu back and that's the God's honest truth.' He looks stricken at the thought of losing Lulu.

Gareth actually seems interested, 'So when was this Norman?'

'Let me see.' he looks up at the ceiling as though

the answer might be written there. 'Must be four weeks ago? Was a Sunday night. I reported it to the police.'

'Four weeks ago, you say? What actually happened?'

Norman takes Gareth step by step through the story of his attack and Lulu's abduction.

I watch Gareth surreptitiously; he appears genuinely interested and I realise what a nice man he is. I take the dishes out into the kitchen and dump them in the sink and run the hot tap on them. They're still chatting when I go back in, so I suggest we go through to the lounge. Gareth sits on the sofa and Norman sits next to him and I take the armchair. Norman continues his story. How long can he go on for?

I zone out again.

'Oh, my goodness!' Norman jumps out of the chair. 'I didn't realise it was so late. I must go, mother will wonder where I am.' A panicked Lulu starts to shake.

'Now don't fret Lulu, don't fret.' He pats her on the head and clips her lead on. I quickly get up and go out into the hall before he changes his mind.

I open the front door and stand aside to let him through.

'Thank you so much Louise. You and the Detective Inspector have made me feel so welcome. This has been one of the best nights of my life.'

'You're very welcome,' I say. 'Anytime. My pleasure.' What am I saying?

'Goodnight Louise.'

'Night, Norman.'

He walks down the path waving; I wave back until

he's out of sight then close the door with a sigh.

Alone at last.

I smooth my floaty top down and moisten my lips. There's a faint rumbling noise coming from the lounge, but I can't quite make out what it is. Ah, Gareth's asleep on the sofa with a snoring Sprocket clamped under his arm. Not surprising really, Gareth must be absolutely shattered. I watch him for a while, he looks so comfortable I don't have the heart to wake him. I run upstairs and grab the quilt from the spare room and gently lay it around him.

I turn out the light and go up to bed.

Chapter Thirteen

'How did it go last night?' Linda asks, grinning at me.

I'm barely through her front door. I close the door and unhook Sprocket's lead and walk through to the kitchen. Linda follows me.

'Well? Spill.'

'Okay.'

'Just okay?'

'Yeah. He stayed the night. He's just left.'

Linda's mouth doesn't exactly drop open but comes pretty close.

'Stayed the night? Hussy.'

'I wish. He fell asleep on the sofa, so I threw a cover over him and went to bed. On my own.'

'Oh.'

'Exactly. And that was after the three of us had dinner, which incidentally wasn't half bad, though I say it myself. Thanks for the recipe.'

'Three of you?'

'Yes. Me, Gareth and the Truth.'

Linda laughs so much I think she's going to choke; her face is bright red and she's actually crying. Sprocket and Henry look at her in alarm, Henry decides he doesn't like it and starts circling her legs, yelping.

Gareth was still asleep when I got up this morning. He didn't look like he'd moved all night; the only difference was that Sprocket had extricated himself from under Gareth's arm and followed me up to bed.

'It's not that funny.'

'It is,' she gasps, 'it really is.'

I wait until she finally stops laughing. Well, she doesn't stop completely, sort of hiccups into laughter now and then.

I cross my arms. 'Anyway, it's your fault.'

'What is?'

'You told the Truth where I live – if you hadn't he wouldn't have turned up and I wouldn't have been lumbered with him.'

'Sorry.' She doesn't look sorry. 'But how did he end up staying for dinner?'

'I felt sorry for him. And before you say anything else I'm going now, or I'll be late for work.'

'Oh, do you have to? Stay a bit longer I want to hear all about it, you've got plenty of time.'

'No. Have to go. See you later.' Small revenge, I'll make her wait.

'I'll look forward to hearing all the gory details.' She calls after me as I close the front door.

'Nothing to tell,' I shout over my shoulder.

Not strictly true.

'What must you think of me?' Gareth had said, blurry eyed, his hair sticking up in tufts. 'I'm so sorry. I'm such a let-down.'

'Doesn't matter,' I'd said, handing him a mug of tea. 'I'd sort of spoilt it anyway, inviting Norman.'

He laughs. 'Yeah, he was a bit of a passion killer, bless him.'

I roll my eyes. 'Me and my big mouth. As you know, I never do know when to shut up.'

'I didn't mind. It was really kind of you. I shouldn't

178

think he gets many invitations to dinner, although obviously I'd rather have you to myself. Join me,' he'd said, throwing open the quilt. So, we had an early morning date, snuggled up on my sofa drinking tea. Deep kisses with early morning breath and tangled hair which shouldn't have been romantic but somehow was. I'd nearly told him then, about the death certificate. It would have been so easy, I felt so close to him, as if I could tell him anything, but then I stopped myself. He was a policeman, would he be compelled to investigate? I couldn't take that risk.

I step out onto the pavement in front of Linda's house and nearly fall over two men struggling to carry a large brown sofa from the back of a huge removal van into the house next door.

'Sorry love,' gasps the man holding the front end of it. His large bald football shaped head is beetroot red and looks like it might explode at any minute. I slide nimbly out of their way and walk back to my house.

There's something niggling at the back of my mind but before I can catch the thought it flutters away. Ever since I found the death certificate my mind has been constantly jumping from one thing to another and I can't seem to concentrate properly. At least when I'm with other people I can think almost normally but when I'm on my own the same thought runs through my mind on a loop.

If Louise Russell is really dead, who the hell am I?

Luckily, I don't have a huge workload, so I manage to look industrious while doing very little. Rupert is desk bound today writing his piece on the Frogham Throttler's latest victim. Sadly, death sells newspapers.

I'm being completely selfish and have barely given Glenda a thought. I'm more concerned with how to find out who I am. I'm desperate to share the fact that I'm dead with someone, but I'm afraid.

What about Dad? What about Nick? Will they both hate me? Will I become a juicy bit of gossip in the newspaper?

I pull an invoice towards me and pretend to study it then tap into Google on my PC. No-one is showing the slightest interest in me, but I feel as if I have guilt written all over my face.

I tap in the date of my death followed by *abduction*; it brings up an episode of Bonanza called Abduction. Great. According to Wikipedia lots of things happened on that date but there's nothing about a baby being abducted. I try the same with kidnap, but the result's the same.

Okay. Maybe it's not on the internet because it was so long ago. I open the password list and look up Rupert's password for the newspaper archives. He's busy writing his article for tonight so he's unlikely to catch me out.

I decide to go straight for the nationals, reasoning that a kidnapped baby would be major news. I'm just about to start when an invoice is slapped on my desk from behind me. Somehow, Bert has walked behind my desk without me realising and is looming over my shoulder. I quickly minimise the screen hoping he hasn't seen what I'm looking at.

'Invoice for payment,' he gasps, out of breath from climbing the stairs from the print room. Hopefully he's too busy trying to breathe to notice what I'm looking at.

'Thanks Bert.'

He eyes the spare chair behind me but before he can sit on it I pick up a file from my desk and plonk it on there. If he sits down, I'll never get rid of him.

'Oi!'

Oh for God's sake, it's Ralph. He's marching purposefully across the office towards me.

'What are you doing up here? I told Lev that he's to bring the invoices up, not you.'

'Sorry Ralph,' gasps Bert.

'You don't need to apologise. I bloody told him and he's ignoring me and I'm not having it.'

I pick up another file and open it and pretend to study it hoping they'll take the hint and go.

'Come on. I'll come downstairs with you, sort him out.'

Ralph marches across the office and Bert lumbers after him, huffing and puffing.

Satisfied they're gone, I maximise my screen and trawl through the newspaper articles, the print is fuzzy in places, so I move my screen a bit closer. Nothing.

Two weeks after my death and I'm just about to give up and there it is: *Baby Abducted from London Garden.*

'You're not on Facebook, are you?'

I jump. For Christ's sake, what now? Ian is standing in front of my desk smirking. He leans over to look at my screen and I quickly minimise it.

He looks disappointed. 'Oh, felt sure you were doing something you shouldn't, you looked far too interested to be working.'

'We're not all like you, Ian.' How many more times am I going to be interrupted? I can come in some days and no one talks to me for the entire day.

'Do you know, they reckon people check their Facebook on average fourteen times day?'

'Is that right.'

'Yeah. So how many times you checked yours today?'

'I'm not on Facebook, I'm working.'

'But that's probably on their phones,' he goes on. 'It's probably less if it's on a PC, unless you work on a PC.'

'I'm working.' GO AWAY.

'Yeah, right.'

I stare at him.

He shrugs. 'I'll go, shall I?'

'Do what you like, I've got work to do. Unlike you.'

He lingers; I watch him impatiently and he eventually saunters off muttering something about the time of the month. Cheeky bastard. I watch him sit down and then wait five minutes just to be sure he doesn't come back. I maximise the screen and zoom in and read.

Four-month-old Veronica Elizabeth Howden was taken from her pram where she was sleeping in the front garden of her home in Ravenscroft Avenue, London, on Wednesday 25th.

Her mother, Elizabeth Howden, had put her outside in her pram for some fresh air and an afternoon nap at approximately 3:15 pm and when she returned to the pram at 4:00pm the baby was gone.

Police are appealing to anyone in the area who may have seen anything suspicious to contact the incident room at Leavens Street or call....

Could it be me? Could it? I scroll through the next week's newspapers; the story is headline news every night but there is nothing, no sightings, no leads.

There's a grainy picture of Elizabeth and Charles Howden but I can't make their features out. Could they be my parents? I scroll through the next few weeks' newspapers. The story gradually gets relegated to the second page, then just a few columns now and then, then nothing.

I go back into Google and type in Veronica Elizabeth Howden. An article from two years ago in the Daily Mail pops up.

Mother who will never give up hope

Baby Veronica Howden was abducted 45 years ago whilst sleeping in her pram in the front garden of her London home. Her mother, Elizabeth Howden, 72, has never given up hope that one day she will be reunited with her first-born child. She and her late husband Charles went on to have three more children, Susan 43, Alison 41 and James 38.

'Charles and I coped in different ways,' she told me. 'Charles chose to think of Veronica as having died whereas I always felt that she was still alive. My hope is that she was taken by someone who would look after her and love her.'

The police operation was one of the largest and longest running but no clues were ever found as to what happened to Veronica. The police investigation has never closed and is still subject to review.

'Of course we never really got over it, but life goes on and we went on to have three more wonderful children. We couldn't let it destroy us, so we carried on. I still have hope.'

The Howden family still live in the same house at Ravenscroft Avenue that they were living in when Veronica was taken. I asked Elizabeth if they hadn't considered moving away for a fresh start after the abduction.

'We thought about it,' she admitted, 'but moving away wouldn't have stopped us grieving for our loss. And also, a part of me hopes that one day she'd come back, or someone would

bring her back, and I wanted to be here if that ever happened.'

A fact that wasn't made public at the time was that when Veronica was taken a stuffed green felt giraffe that was in her pram was also taken. For this reason, Elizabeth is so sure Veronica was taken by someone who would look after her; she believes they took the toy for Veronica to keep.

My heart's pounding; I'm going to have a heart attack. I can't breathe.

Raffy.

A green, felt giraffe that I went to bed with every night. I still have him, worn and frayed, he lives on top of my chest of drawers, away from Sprocket's eager paws.

'LOUISE!'

Ralph swims into view. He's at the front of my desk with a concerned look on his face.

'You alright girl? You're as white as a sheet.'

'Umm, no, not really,' my voice is shaky. 'Not feeling very well.'

Don't cry. Don't.

'You look bleeding awful, get yourself off home.'

'I think I will.' I'm already logging out of my PC.

'You sure you're okay to drive? I can give you a lift home you know.'

I shake my head not trusting myself to speak.

I pick up my bag and tuck it under my arm, my legs feel shaky when I stand up, but I put my head up and look Ralph straight in the eye.

'I'll be fine Ralph, honest. Just a bad migraine, I'll take some tablets and have a lie down and I'll be right as rain tomorrow.'

He gives me a look that tells me he doesn't believe a word of it and as I walk out of the office I can feel him watching me. I don't look at anyone else, just keep going. If I can just hold it together for a bit longer, just a flight of stairs and then I can get into my car and crumble.

But I don't.

I get into the car and my breathing gradually returns to normal and my hands stop shaking. I look at myself in the mirror and I look a bit pale but otherwise okay. My mouth has set in a grim line.

I start the ignition and put the car into reverse.

I want some answers.

I'm going to see Dad.

'Oh, hello.' Sister Kathy is surprised to see me, I don't usually visit at this time on a weekday. 'Your Dad's just having his lunch, but he shouldn't be long.'

'No worries, I'll wait in the day room.' I plaster a fake smile on my face, but I don't think I'm fooling her. I walk quickly away before she can say anything. As soon as Dad's finished I'm going to take him round to his room. I don't want anyone overhearing our conversation. That's supposing I can get any sense out of him.

I wait impatiently wandering from window to notice board and back again. I'm probably wasting my time, but I have to try to get some answers.

Dad comes out of the dining room and I make a beeline for him. He jumps when I link my arm in his and propel him down the corridor to his room.

'Oh, hello love.' He looks startled. At least he seems to recognise me today.

I walk him quickly through the doorway into his room and sit him down in his chair by the window. I go back and close the door. I need to calm down, I'm not going to get any answers by agitating him.

'What did you have for lunch, Dad? Was it nice?' I sound false even to myself.

'Sausage and mash. Was okay.' This doesn't bode well as I saw the menu on the way in and the choice was shepherd's pie or ravioli. If he can't remember what he had for lunch he's hardly going to remember something that happened forty-five years ago.

We sit in silence for a while and I wonder how I'm going to start the conversation. *Hey Dad you know you keep saying I'm not your daughter, well now I know why,* or maybe, *do you want to tell me why I'm dead?*

'Look at that tiger up that tree, it'll never get down you know.'

He's looking through the window at the tree in the courtyard. It's a spindly sapling which would struggle to hold a bird.

'No, he won't,' I say.

I clear my throat. 'Dad,' my voice is a bit wobbly. 'Do you remember a street called Ravenscroft Avenue?'

'I don't think they should have tigers in gardens. It's not safe. What if they got out and attacked someone? You wouldn't stand a chance.'

'Dad,' I try again, 'Ravenscroft Avenue? Do you remember it?'

'And,' he goes on, 'they're a magnificent beast and they'd have to be shot if they escaped. No, it's definitely not right.'

'DAD,' I yell, and he looks at me. 'Do you remember, a long, long time ago, a baby was abducted? When I was three months old?'

'Although it doesn't look bothered, that tiger, seems to quite like it up that tree.'

'Dad, did you have a baby called Louise who died?

Did you take someone else's baby?' I'm trying to keep my voice low, I don't want anyone else to hear.

'Perhaps it's cooler up there.' He nods at the tree. 'Out of the heat.'

It was a stupid idea. Pointless. I may as well go home. I think I knew it wasn't going to work; he's so confused, he doesn't even know where he is most of the time.

'Yes, Dad he probably likes the view up there.' This seems to please Dad and he nods in agreement. We sit in silence and both of us gaze out of the window.

'Would you like a cup of tea?' Dad waits for me to answer.

'Yes, that would be lovely,' I say, absently. I would love a cup of tea, but I don't think I'll be getting one.

'Put the kettle on then and we'll make a pot.' He grins. There's a glimpse of my old dad there.

'I'll go and get us one.' I stand up, 'I won't be long.'

I have my hand on the door handle when he suddenly starts to speak.

'Your mother was a good woman you know, she only ever wanted to do the right thing.' He leans forward in his chair.

I stay quiet not wanting to interrupt him, though I offer a smile and nod of encouragement as I sit back down

'She used to walk for miles, round and round the streets. Day after day. As if it would make her forget. We just couldn't make sense of it. Thought we'd done something wrong. Didn't matter what the doctors said, we blamed ourselves.'

He has a faraway look in his eyes, reminiscing. I

daren't breathe, in case it stops him. I pray that no-one interrupts us.

'You were crying, and she picked you up to comfort you because you were on your own, outside. That's all she meant to do. Comfort you.' He speaks in a matter of fact way, reliving a memory. 'But before she knew what she'd done she was back home.' He pauses and stares at me. 'With you.' He pats my hand. 'She didn't mean to do it but then it was too late. Too late.' He shakes his head, 'I should have insisted but I couldn't. She was heartbroken, and I think if I'd taken you back I'd have lost her forever. And then we moved a week later and that was that.' He folds his arms across his body and turns back to looking out of the window.

This is what I suspected. This is what I feared. It must be true. Even in his confused state Dad cannot have just made this up.

I feel numb.

'That tiger's gone now. Someone must have helped it down.'

'Yes, it's gone Dad.'

'Good.' He looks at me with a big smile. 'Do you know, I feel quite relieved about that. Shall we get that cup of tea now?'

'Good idea.'

He gets up and we walk back round to the lounge; our timing is perfect. Liz, the care assistant, is serving drinks from a battered tea trolley and her face lights up when she sees us.

'Thomas! Your usual is it? White tea with one sugar? And what would you like Lynn?'

'White tea, no sugar, please Liz. And it's Louise, not Lynn.' Or maybe it's Veronica.

188

Dad settles down on the sofa and I walk back over to the trolley to pick up the teas.

'There you are Lynn, the one on the right is sugared.'

'Louise.'

She shrugs.

'My name's Louise. If I can remember your name Liz, I'm sure you can remember mine.'

She looks at me with a shocked expression as I pick up the teas. I think she'll remember it now.

'I'm sorry, Liz. That was rude of me.' I shouldn't have taken it out on her.

She smiles, but the sides of her mouth twitch and I don't think she's going to forgive me for snapping at her.

As I come out of Blossom Unit, I rummage in my bag for my phone and see that I've missed a call from Nick.

'Hi Nick. You rang?'

'Hi Sis, how's things?'

'Okay. Just been to see Dad.'

'Have you?' He sounds surprised. 'Thought you'd be at work.'

'Day off.' Why am I lying?

'Pulled a sickie, have you?' He laughs.

'Something like that.'

'You okay? You don't sound like my normal bolshie sister.'

I swallow, unable to speak. I could say but I'm not your sister; I'm not who you think I am. I want to tell him, I want to share this horrible secret so badly with someone, so that I don't feel so alone but I can't. I can't destroy everything he's ever known, it's bad enough that every part of my life feels like a lie. How would he feel about me if he knew?

'I'm fine. Difficult visit with Dad that's all, nothing serious. What were you ringing for anyway?'

'To let you know I'm away working for a week, off to Paris on a fashion shoot.'

'Lucky you. Nice work if you can get it.'

'It'll be a ball ache, shit food and stroppy Frogs. Can't go quick enough for me.'

'Poor thing.'

'I know it's a hard life. But seriously, I know it's not a great time to be away and I'm just ringing to say sorry I won't be around, but you can always ring me.'

'No worries.'

'I saw the news about Glenda. Terrible. Poor woman.'

'Did you see the news, or did Linda tell you?' I ask. 'What with you being so friendly and all?'

Nick is quiet for a moment, I can almost hear him thinking.

'Yeah, we've been chatting.'

'I know. Remember what I said Nick, don't mess her about, she's my friend.'

'I won't. I really like her, Lou. She's *normal*.'

Despite my misery I laugh. 'Watch it Nick. Sounds like you're hooked.'

He laughs but doesn't deny it. We chat for a while longer then hang up. I start the car up and I rest my hands on the steering wheel and take a few deep breaths. I wish I felt normal. I feel like I'm dragging a huge bird of doom on my shoulders and I can't see how to shake it off. The great oozelum bird of doom as Nick calls it; the great oozelum bird of doom flies around in ever decreasing circles until it disappears up its own arsehole. Just how I feel.

I wish fervently that I'd never found that death certificate because then I'd never have known.

Ignorance *is* bliss.

'You're early,' Linda opens the front door to me and I follow her in.

'Yeah, had the dentists so sloped off a bit early.' The lie trips easily off my tongue and it makes me wonder how Mum and Dad managed to live a lie for all those years. How did they do it? Knowing that their whole life was based on a lie? How could they cope with the thought of being found out at any time? Or does it get easier with time? Perhaps they convinced themselves it never happened. Maybe that's what I need to do.

Sprocket is jumping up for attention, so I kneel down and scratch his ears while he tries to lick my face. He doesn't care who I am. I follow Linda into the kitchen and leave Sprocket to go back to lying by the front door on the cool tiles.

A rosy cheeked, cheerful looking lady is seated at Linda's table, mug of tea in hand.

'Sarah, this is my friend Lou, Lou this is my new next-door neighbour, Sarah.'

Short, round with wispy chestnut hair and a flushed face, Sarah gets up and puts out her hand.

'Hello Lou, nice to meet you.'

'You too, how're you settling in?'

'Oh, you know.' She grimaces, sitting back down. 'Exhausting but just relieved to be in at last. Linda's been very kindly providing us all with cups of tea. We've done the move ourselves so lots of thirsty friends and relatives around.'

'It's nice to have neighbours at last,' says Linda, 'the house has been empty for too long.' She doesn't mention the noises or that she thinks it's haunted.

'I think I met one of your helpers this morning, carrying a sofa.'

'Oh, that was my husband, Ronnie. He's still cursing that sofa– nearly did his back in.'

'At least you're in now, you can take your time getting sorted.'

'True. The house is a bit dated, but we'll work through it all gradually. Not in any hurry. It's sort of retro in its own way. I'd forgotten what hard work it was finding the right house, but we got there in the end. The estate agent was brilliant – it was a bit of a funny one as the house was an inheritance. Three brothers who could never agree on anything apparently.' Sarah takes a slurp of tea, 'Men,' she says, rolling her eyes.

There's that niggle at the back of my mind again, but before I can grab it, it floats off.

'I must get back, I'll be in the doghouse for not doing my share.' She drains her cup.

'She seems nice,' I say to Linda as the door closes behind Sarah.

'She is. Met her husband briefly and he seems nice too – not as bubbly as her though. I'm just glad it's not empty anymore, gave me the willies. Anyway, how was the dentists?'

I look at her blankly for a moment then remember my lie. That's the trouble with lying - you need a good memory.

'Oh, fine, just a check-up.'

'You stopping for a coffee?'

'No, I won't, thanks. Going to pop home and

change then take Sprocket for a walk. Shall I call for you on the way?'

'Good idea, leave him here and I'll get him harnessed up ready. Half an hour?'

'Yeah, that'll be great. Won't be long.'

I let myself out of the front door; next door's 'For sale' sign has found its way into Linda's garden, so I pick it up and lean over the wall and prop it next to their gate.

I swing my arms and take deep breaths and put my shoulders back; positive mental attitude. I march back to my house repeating 'everything will be alright' to myself.

And it suddenly hits me. Bang, just like that, I remember where I've seen Suzanne Jenkins, the first murder victim, before.

Chapter Fourteen

I rang work this morning and asked if I could take the rest of the week off as holiday even though it was short notice. I said that I had stuff that I needed to sort out for Dad. Ralph was so kind, said of course it wasn't a problem but that no way was I going to take holiday, I could just have the week off.

I nearly cried and felt rotten for lying, although I suppose it wasn't a complete lie. I have a meeting at the hospital on Thursday about Dad.

Or I could, a mischievous little voice says, give him the scoop of a lifetime...*stolen child from 45 years ago found in Frogham*. I shudder, a vision of my photograph and story splashed all over the front page. What would Nick think? Would my friends still want to be my friends or would it all be too weird for them? The nationals would be sure to pick it up and before you know it we'd have satellite vans all over the precinct and reporters beating a path to my door. It doesn't bear thinking about.

Gareth rang at nine o'clock last night, apologetic and sounding exhausted, to say that he couldn't leave work but would hopefully see me tonight. I was desperately disappointed at not seeing him but also relieved in case I blurted out that I'm really Veronica Howden.

Of course, the minute he hung up I remembered I

was supposed to tell him where I'd seen Suzanne Jenkins. I must tell him tonight.

By the time I went to bed I felt mentally and physically exhausted and I fell asleep instantly, but it didn't last. I woke up at three o'clock absolutely wide awake and knew there was no possibility of going back to sleep. I got up and dozed fitfully on the sofa watching catch up TV. I may as well have been watching soup because I couldn't even tell you what I watched.

So, here I am at Dad's house. I felt compelled to come here but I don't know why and I'm sitting on the bed in Dad's bedroom, Sprocket fast asleep next to me. I've been through all the chest of drawers and wardrobes and found nothing. I don't even know what I'm looking for. I've been here for nearly three hours and been through all the rooms. There's nothing *to* find; I know what happened, Dad told me and it all makes a horrible kind of sense. The real Louise died at three months old and Mum stole me from Elizabeth Howden's garden to replace the baby she lost.

Why did they keep the death certificate? There is nothing else in the house that is incriminating in any way, so why keep that? The only thing I can think of is that maybe Mum and Dad couldn't throw it away because they'd be denying that the real Louise Russell ever existed. Who knows?

They got away with the perfect crime. They moved here from London and nobody suspected, but why would they? Mum and Dad hardly looked like master criminals. If Dad had taken me back, would the police have been sympathetic? I don't know. Does it matter now?

The real question is: what do I do about it?

My real mother. Elizabeth Howden. Do I look like her? I have brother and sisters that I've never met, and I can't help being curious. What sort of life would I have had? I'm happy but would my life have been different? What was my real father like? A father that I will never know because that he's dead.

If I could go back in time I wouldn't look under that drawer, I wouldn't open that envelope and find my own death certificate. But I know now, and I can't un-know it.

I really only have two choices; I either come out in the open and the world will know I'm not really Louise Russell. If I do this it'll ruin what's left of Dad's life, devastate Nick and ruin Mum's memory.

Or I keep the secret. And tell no-one, ever.

I want to keep it a secret, but I don't know if I can. I need to talk about it. But if I know one thing about secrets it's that if you tell one person then it's not a secret anymore.

Although there is someone I can tell who'll never tell a soul.

'Sprocket.' I stroke his ears and he opens his eyes sleepily, 'I have a secret to tell you.' Before I can speak he jumps up from the bed barking, spooked by the clang of the letterbox. He races downstairs to see what the postman's left. I plod down after him and pick up the three letters from the floor. He looks at me expectantly.

'They're not for you, you wally. They're letters.' I wave them at him and he looks at me dumbly, head cocked on one side, tongue hanging out. I leaf through them, they're not for Dad either. Mr & Mrs Harper, Dad's next-door neighbours. I'll pop round with them and if they're in I'll let them know how Dad is, he was very friendly with Simon.

I slip my shoes on, pick up my keys and leave an annoyed Sprocket sitting in the hallway.

'Won't be long.' He ignores me, I think he's sulking.

I tramp down the drive and round the hedge and up the Harpers' driveway. Their house isn't quite as big as Dad's, but has a lovely big bay window. They've probably lived there for thirty odd years and must have been young when they moved in although they've always seemed old to me, yet they're probably not much older than I am. I have vague memories of them, they always used to come in and see the new year in with Mum and Dad and when Mum died Dad started going to them instead. I think they even came to my wedding; how awful that I can't remember.

The curtains are closed across the bay window and there's no car on the drive. I ring the doorbell just in case and can hear the faint sound of Westminster chimes from within.

I think I see a shadow moving through the frosted glass in the door, so I ring again.

The door opens very slowly and a white curly head pops around the door. My first thought is that she must be a midget but as she pulls the door open I realise that she's in a wheelchair. Dad must have told me why, but I can't for the life of me remember. I wish I'd properly listened to Dad now. Another regret.

'Hello Louise, nice to see you.' She smiles showing small yellowing teeth. I've never seen someone with skin so pale, baby like.

'Hello.' I desperately try to remember her name

but my memory fails me. 'The postman put your post through Dad's door so I've just brought it round.' I hold out the letters to her.

'Oh, thank you, that's kind of you. Would you like to come in?' She's saying the words but I have the definite feeling that she doesn't want me to accept.

'Oh no, I won't thanks, got a lot on.'

'I see,' she sounds relieved. 'How's Tom doing?'

'He's okay, being looked after. They're still not sure what's wrong with him, so can't treat him yet. I'm sure once he's diagnosed they'll soon have him better.'

'Oh dear, poor Tom. Simon really misses him you know – he was asking if he'd be able to visit him. I'd visit myself but it's not so easy now I'm confined to this.' She taps her hands on the wheelchair.

'Well maybe once they've sorted him out. They're advising family only at the moment,' I say with a jollity I don't feel.

'If we can do anything at all just let us know. Simon'll be home any minute for his lunch so if you think of anything just let us know.'

'I will, thanks. Give Simon my regards.' As I turn to walk away she's already closed the door. What an odd sort, bag of nerves, why would you close your curtains in the middle of the day? She must be sitting in semi-darkness. Like a vampire. Maybe that's why she's so pale. Simon's car pulls past me onto their drive and I give a jolly wave that I don't feel and carry on back into Dad's.

I've searched the house. For what? I have no idea. May as well go out and have a look in the shed as well, and be done with it.

'Come on Sprocket.' He looks up at me

expectantly and I harness him up and clip his lead on. Don't want him vanishing into the outback.

I rummage around amongst assorted debris in the kitchen drawer for the back-door key and wonder why I'm bothering. I suppose I owe it to Dad, he was obsessed with the shed, so I ought to check it. I find a bunch of keys and unlock the door, hoping that one of the bunch is the key to the shed.

Out in the garden it's still hot but overcast and oppressive, a promise of rain in the air. The grass is overgrown and needs cutting; a job for Nick next time he comes. The path to the shed is crazy paved but the moss is taking over and will soon have covered all the paving. We pick our way along the path and before we reach the shed I loop Sprocket's lead over a branch of the apple tree to stop him wandering off while I try the keys.

Five minutes later and I've tried every key on the bunch; not one of them fits. I should have got Nick to get the bolt cutters on it while he was here. I could look in the garage for them, but I don't have a clue where the key to the garage is either.

'Well, that was a waste of time,' I say to Sprocket.

He looks up at me and whines, he's backed himself as far away from the shed as he can get, and his lead is stretched tight. The sky darkens, and I hear the low rumble of distant thunder. Sprocket growls and I wrap my arms around myself, a sudden chill in the air.

I have a horrible feeling that I'm not alone; that I'm being watched. I look around the garden, but it's so overgrown a whole army could be hiding in it.

I walk over to Sprocket and try to unloop his lead. He's pulled it so tight I can't undo it with my fingers and my hands start to shake.

199

'Come here, Sprock, I can't undo you.' He looks up at me but doesn't move. I yank the lead and he digs his paws into the ground. I feel panic rising and tell myself not to be so stupid, but my fingers won't work, and I can't unhook him.

It grows even darker and Sprocket squashes himself further into the tree trunk, growling and baring his teeth. I stop pretending I'm not frightened and decide to unclip his lead and drag him into the house by his harness. As I lean over him and fumble to unclip him a shadow falls over us and I realise that we're not alone.

I slowly straighten up, my stomach is churning, my mouth is dry and I turn around holding the bunch of keys around my knuckles as a weapon. I'm looking straight at a denim shirt stretched across a massive chest. I gulp and crane my neck to look up into the face of Brendan, Dad's taxi driver, next-door neighbour.

'Oh, hello.' his face breaks into a smile. 'Hope I didn't make you jump.'

Relief floods my body and I feel light headed and spaced out.

'I was hoping to catch you,' he goes on. 'Wanted a quiet word.' He bends down to Sprocket and rubs him under the ears. 'Hello mate, what's your name?'

'Sprocket,' I say. Sprocket's tail is wagging now, whatever was frightening him, it wasn't Brendan. 'What did you want a word about?' I don't sound very friendly. I don't feel very friendly.

'Yeah, well, the thing is,' he looks uncomfortable. 'Is Tom not well? Only I've not seen him for a while and I was just a bit concerned.'

'No, he's not well. He's in hospital and they're

keeping him in for a while. For tests. They're not really sure what's wrong with him.'

'I'm sorry to hear that. Poor Tom. Hope they can get him better.'

'Thanks.'

'Look. I won't beat about the bush, I guessed as much. I was thinking – would you like me to cut the grass? Just while he's in hospital? Be a shame to let the garden get too overgrown.'

'Oh. Um. I couldn't ask you to do that, but it's very kind of you.'

'You didn't ask, I offered. And it would help me as well.'

'How would it help you?'

'Well, that's why I wanted a quiet word. The garden's a security risk to be honest.'

I look at him doubtfully.

'I used to be in security and this garden makes a nice screen for someone up to no good.'

Security? He's the right size for a bouncer.

'I used to run a security company in the Middle East before I semi-retired.'

So not a bouncer.

'And,' he goes on, 'I think someone has been prowling around the garden because I've definitely seen someone in here. But they're clever; I've never managed to catch them.'

'Was that when my Dad was here?'

'Yes, a few times.'

Poor Dad. We didn't believe him.

'I didn't say anything to Tom because I didn't want to alarm him. But I don't know how they're getting in. Or out.'

I make a decision to trust Brendan. I hope I won't

regret it.

'Have you got a crowbar or bolt cutters, Brendan?'

He looks surprised. 'Yes. Why?'

'Do you think you could get that padlock off the shed for me?'

He smiles. 'Of course, no problem, I'll go and get some tools.'

He tramps off across the garden and squeezes through a gap in the bushes into his garden. So that's how he got in; Dad didn't imagine seeing him, he just mistook his motives. I hope.

A few minutes later Brendan reappears with a crowbar in his hand.

'This should do it.' He inserts the end through the shed hasp. 'You sure about this?'

'I'm sure.'

Brendan gets his weight behind the crowbar and the wood cracks and splinters as he levers on it. A loud crack and the padlock and hasp lie on the floor and the door swings open. Sprocket whines.

'Don't start again.' I shoot him a warning look and he lies down on the floor as far away from the shed as his lead will allow.

Right. Let's see what's in that shed.

I step over the padlock and look inside.

It's empty.

Sprocket and I trudge up to the Rise. The threatened rain is still a threat; the sky getting darker and darker, the heat more and more oppressive.

I don't know what I expected to find in the shed, but I did expect to find *something*. But it was completely empty, even the floor was swept clean. The last time I remember seeing it – which was years and years ago – it was a jumble of old lawn mowers and assorted pots and gardening implements, bags of compost and assorted bits and pieces. Where's it all gone? Brendan had looked at me with a quizzical expression on his face and all I could do was shrug.

Dad must have cleared it out then forgotten he'd done it.

Brendan managed to bang the hasp back on and wedge a twig to hold it closed so it didn't swing open in the wind. He promised to cut the grass although I said he really didn't need to. He seemed to think he could get his lawn mower through the gap in the hedge, although I have my doubts. But then again, he fits through and he's massive.

I look down despondently at Sprocket and he gazes up at me mournfully.

'What are we like eh Sprock? A couple of miseries.'

I haven't heard anything from Gareth so I'm guessing he can't get away from work. I consider texting him but stop myself; don't want to look too keen. Although I am. Very.

A giant raindrop lands on my head. Here it comes, we're going to get drowned. I run for the trees dragging a reluctant Sprocket behind me. I know it's dangerous and with the luck I'm having I'll probably get struck by lightning but hey, bring it on.

We just make it before the heavens open and the rain comes lashing down in stair rods; rain so heavy that I can only just make out a figure running towards me. Is it the Frogham Throttler? Am I about to become the third victim? Sprocket spots him too and despite the rain his tail starts to wag. I let go of the breath that I didn't realise I was holding.

'Misjudged that!' Gareth says laughingly as he joins

me under the tree, 'Guessed you'd be here so thought I'd surprise you.'

I look up at him; his hair is wet and his eyelashes glisten with water. He looks utterly gorgeous.

He puts his arms around me and pulls me close.

'Are you surprised to see me?'

'I am.' And Sprocket is too, he runs around us in excited circles and wraps his lead around our legs until we're tied together.

I snuggle into him and drink in the smell of musky aftershave and wet shirt.

'We may have to stay like this all night if it doesn't stop raining.'

'We might,' I agree.

'Or,' he says, nuzzling my neck, 'we might have to make a run for it and go back to yours and get out of these wet clothes.'

'We might.'

'It doesn't look like it's going to stop.'

'It doesn't.'

'I think we should make a run for it.'

'We should.'

Gareth unwraps the lead from around our legs and untangles Sprocket.

'You ready?'

'I'm ready.'

'RUN!'

He grabs hold of my hand and we start to run but I can't keep up with Gareth's giant strides.

'C'mon! How can you take such small steps?'

I start to giggle which makes me run even slower. I let go of Sprocket's lead and he races off home.

'C'mon shortarse get a move on!'

'I'm not short I'm five foot seven,' I shout as we

turn the corner into my street. Sprocket is already sitting outside the front door.

Gareth suddenly stops, and I nearly fall over him.

'We're nearly there, keep going!'

He ignores me and bends down, grabs hold of my legs and swings me over his shoulder in a fireman's lift.

'Put me down!' I'm screaming and laughing as he runs down the street with me. He swings me down outside my front door and the three of us stand under the porch listening to the rain pounding down around us.

Gareth pushes my soaked hair out of my eyes.

'Did I ever tell you I like the dishevelled look?'

'You may have mentioned it.' Which is just as well since I seem to sport that look more often than not.

He pulls me close to him and our coats squelch together making the most unromantic farting noise.

And then we kiss. A long, deep, sweet kiss.

After what seems like forever we both come up for air.

'Should we go in?' I suggest.

'I think we should.'

I manage to retrieve the key from my coat pocket and open the door and we fall into the lounge and collapse in a giggling heap on the sofa. Sprocket then jumps all over us adding muddy paws to our sodden clothes.

'Since when was getting caught in the rain so much fun?' I can hardly speak for laughing.

'It never was fun until I met you.' The mood has suddenly changed, the air seems charged. Gareth smooths his hand over my face, wiping away the rain.

'I should arrest you for looking so gorgeous.' He

gives an embarrassed laugh, 'And I should arrest myself for spouting such a cheesy line.'

'You should, but I'm not complaining.'

'Do you think that you know when you've met your soul mate?' He's suddenly serious. 'Because I think I've met mine.'

I stare at him; I so want to believe he means me but feel I should look behind me in case he's talking to someone else.

'Do you?' I say stupidly, 'Who's your soul mate?'

'You,' he says, gathering me in his arms. 'You.'

'Does Sprocket always sleep with you?'

'Most of the time.' I lay my head on his chest. 'Except when he sleeps with random policemen on the sofa downstairs.'

He laughs. 'Not my finest moment was it?'

'Oh I don't know, you passed the test – if you don't pass the Sprocket test then it's a no go I'm afraid.'

Sprocket raises his head from the bottom of the bed, he knows we're talking about him and he's not impressed. He's sulking because he spent last night in the kitchen and not on the bed. Well, there are limits, some things that a dog shouldn't witness.

'I'm going to have to go. Duty calls.'

'Must you?'

'Fraid so. I don't want to, believe me. Don't you have to go to work?'

'Couple of days off,' I lie, 'holidays to use up.'

'I'm jealous, wish I could stay here all day. In bed with you.'

I snuggle closer. 'You could stay a bit longer.'

He groans. 'Don't tempt me. I need to go back to

mine for some clean clothes, I can hardly turn up in last night's.'

True. They're still in a heap on the lounge floor, wet, crumpled and muddy. That sofa's going to take a bit of cleaning too.

He reluctantly pulls away from me and slides out of bed.

'Be back in a minute.'

He reappears minutes later dressed in last night's crumpled and muddy clothes.

'Nice look,' I say.

He pulls a face. 'They're still wet too. We should have hung them up to dry.'

'We should. Wasn't really in the mood for housework though.'

'No, nor me. Much better things to do.' He grins wolfishly.

'Well Detective Inspector, I do believe you're flirting with me.' I say in my best southern belle accent.

'Wish I didn't have to go.'

'So stay.'

'I can't. I have to go.' He leans over the bed and we kiss, neither of us wanting to break away.

I push him away. 'Go,' I say. 'Go catch the throttler. But come back soon.'

'Just try and stop me.'

Chapter Fifteen

'Stay away from the shed. It's dangerous.'

'I'll stay away. Now stop worrying and go and eat your tea.'

'Promise me.'

'I promise Dad. Honestly you don't need to worry.'

He's looking at me but I can tell he's not listening. Since we came back to his room he's been agitated and upset. I thought maybe it was because of the meeting, but he hasn't even mentioned it. He didn't seem that bothered when we were in there – didn't even ask what the meeting was for. He's been complaining of being cold, so I told him I'd bring some jumpers in and that's what started it. He doesn't want me to go to his house, keeps saying there's danger there.

I give him a hug. 'I'll see you soon Dad.'

'Stay here. With me.'

I laugh. 'I'm not allowed Dad. Besides they don't have any spare beds.'

'You can have my bed. I'll sleep in the chair. It's safe here.'

'I'll be fine, stop worrying.'

'Danger. There's danger. Betty agrees with me. She's very worried about you.'

The clairvoyant's message from Mum comes back

to me. It's just nonsense. Isn't it?

'I'm fine Dad.'

'I don't think you are, you've got a lot to think about and that's what worries me. You're not concentrating and that's when it's most dangerous, that's when it happens.'

'What happens, Dad? What do I have to be careful of?'

'I don't know!' he almost wails, 'I just know that there's danger, it's all mixed up but if I could just think clearly I could tell you, but it's so hard.'

He's looking at me intently, I almost tell him that I've already opened the shed and it's empty but stop myself; it might make him worse.

'Look I won't go. I'll wait until Nick's back at the weekend and go with him.'

'Promise?'

'I promise. Now go and get your tea before it's all gone.' I have my fingers crossed my fingers behind my back.

He doesn't move and as I walk out of the ward I look back and he's still watching me. I put my hand up and wave, but he doesn't move. I carry on out into the car park but don't look back again.

Once outside I pull my mobile out and ring Nick; he's still in Paris but I promised him I'd ring as soon as the meeting was over. He answers on the first ring.

'Hi Sis, how did it go?'

'Horrible. I didn't expect so many people to be there.'

'Really?'

'Yeah, there was the psychiatrist, psychologist, Sister Kathy, the liaison officer and even the care assistant, Liz.'

'Bloody hell, that must have been intimidating.'

'Well no, it wasn't really, they were all so nice. They asked Dad in to start with and asked him how he thought he was getting on. He said he thought he was a bit better, especially now he's got his old cabin back. He said he hoped it wasn't going to take too long as he had to get back to work.' Dad had looked so old and frail when he came in, hard to believe he could age so quickly. I just wanted to scoop him up and take him home.

'So he doesn't think he's in a hotel anymore?'

'No. He thinks he's in the Navy and he's on a ship. Mum is also on a ship off the coast of Africa and uses the ship's radio to talk to him every day.'

'Christ. Where does all that come from?'

'I don't know. He couldn't remember who I was to start with but then he did after a while. He asked where you were, I told him you were abroad and couldn't get away.'

'I wish I could have been there.'

'I know. I'm not trying to make you feel guilty, just telling you how it was. He also said you were getting married.'

'What?!'

'Yeah, said you were getting married to a policewoman.'

Nick laughs. 'Where does he get it from?'

'Tom's world, I don't know. It's weird, he seems to pick stuff up somehow and then jumble it up. I haven't mentioned that I'm seeing Gareth or that you're seeing Linda but somehow he knows, but gets it all mixed up.'

'I'm not...'

'Don't bother denying it. Anyway, our loves lives

don't matter, it's just strange how on some level he seems to know stuff that he shouldn't.'

'It is weird, I've noticed it before on other things.'

'Maybe,' I say, 'as he's losing his faculties other senses take over. I don't know.'

'That's a bit deep, Lou.'

'I know, tell me to shut up.'

'Shut up. Have they decided on a diagnosis? Can they treat him and get him better?'

'Well, after he'd gone they told me that they've been observing him and doing memory and cognitive tests on him, oh, and also they've done a couple of scans which I didn't know about to rule out a physical cause.'

Nick is silent, so I carry on. 'They said he has *Parkinson's*, but I've never noticed Dad shaking or anything like that but they said he has symptoms of it. And they can't give a definite diagnosis as there's no test for it, but they're pretty sure he's got a form of dementia. Something called Lewy Bodies.'

'Shit.'

'Exactly. There isn't really any treatment for it, apparently people with that type of dementia don't respond well to medication.'

'Makes them worse,' says Nick, 'can even be fatal.'

'What? How do you know?' I'm shocked, 'I've never even heard of it.'

'Been Googling Dad's symptoms and it all fitted; delusions, seeing things, not recognising people. Rapid onset. I was hoping like hell he didn't have it, but I'm not surprised.'

'Why didn't you tell me what you thought? You never said anything.'

'Could have been wrong, couldn't I? And to be

honest Lou, what was the point? I've read so much about dementia and I wish I hadn't because there's fuck all in the way of treatment for Lewy Bodies. Nothing to slow it down. Nothing.'

He's right. That's pretty much what the psychiatrist said. No treatment. No hope. Oh, they tried to paint a more optimistic picture but realistically Dad's only going to get worse.

'So what happens now? What do we do?' Nick sounds desolate.

'We don't have to do anything yet. They still want to monitor him, make sure of their diagnosis. If they confirm it, they'll have to draw up a schedule of his needs as he obviously won't be able to go home but he'll need to go to a care home that can cope with him. They haven't given us a deadline or anything. They said not to concern ourselves at the moment, they'll give us plenty of notice.'

'Poor Dad.'

I don't say anything; I'm too choked to speak. A snapshot of the future; Dad in a care home, getting worse and worse. Unbearable. And the practicalities of it all, the house and everything in it – what are we going to do with it all? I push it to the back of my mind, one thing at a time.

'Okay. Look, I'll be back the day after tomorrow, so we can decide what we'll do then. I think we should just try and get our heads around it and not think ahead too far or we'll drive ourselves mad.'

'Okay,' I say in a small voice.

'Are you going home now?'

'Yeah, just have to pick Sprocket up from Linda's.'

'Maybe you should stay there, not be on your own. You've had a shock.'

'I won't be on my own.'

'Why's that? Is there something you're not telling me?'

'You're a crap liar, Nick.' I laugh.

'What?' he says, affecting mock innocence.

'I know you've been talking to Linda, so you know all about Gareth.'

'Yeah, can't lie. What's he like then, this plod? Is he good enough for my sister?'

'He's gorgeous and he's definitely good enough.' I feel warm and fuzzy just talking about him, the memory of Tuesday night still fresh. How can one part of me feel so happy and the other so miserable? Perhaps that's what I should do; compartmentalise my feelings. Three compartments: one for the happy Louise, one for the sad Louise who's losing her Dad inch by inch and, one box for the dead Louise. Maybe I could put that one away and never get it out again. Forget about it. Bury it. Perhaps I could get myself hypnotised and delete it.

'I need to meet him, check him out.'

'You will.'

'Perhaps this weekend?'

'We'll see,' I say. 'He might not be about, he's running a murder investigation.'

'It'll take more than murder to stop me from meeting him. But seriously Lou, I'm happy for you.'

'Me too.'

I hear voices in the background, someone calling Nick's name.

'Gotta go Sis, Frogs are calling. See you Saturday.'

'Yep, see you Saturday.'

I start to put my phone in my bag then remember that I didn't tell Gareth about my sighting of Suzanne

Jenkins. Probably not important at all as it must have been about a week before she went missing. But still. Should report it. I call Gareth's number and it goes straight to voicemail.

I put my phone away. I'll tell him later.

I walk back to the car and get in and start it up.

But hang on, I'll forget. How many times have I been going to tell him and forgotten?

I'm sure it's not important but I should tell him. I pull my phone out of my bag and ring him. It goes straight to voicemail, so I leave a message.

There. Job done.

But there's still that niggle.

Something else. Something just out of reach that vanishes when I try to catch it.

It'll come back to me.

'How did the meeting go?'

We're sitting in Linda's kitchen, Sprocket and Henry are snoozing under the table and Linda and I are tucking into cheese toasties.

I tell her.

'Oh. I'm so sorry. I don't know what to say. Your poor Dad.'

I nod.

'At least your mum's been spared it, although I know that's not much consolation. And you say he doesn't seem unhappy?'

'No, he's not unhappy, seems quite content in his own little world. The psychiatrist said that his world is as real to him as this one is to us; he only seems to get distressed when he pops back to our world for a while. He can't make sense of it.' And eventually he'll forget everything, all about the abduction and I'll be

214

the only person in the world who knows the truth.

I have a sudden urge to tell Linda everything; the abduction, my death certificate, the lot. Unburden myself. But I don't. 'He's got so frail, the weight's dropping off him. Says he's feeling the cold. And it's not even cold, it's summer.'

'Is he not eating?'

'Yeah, he's got a good appetite, but the weight is still coming off, the doctors say that's all part of Lewy Bodies, but it doesn't make sense to me. If he's eating why is he losing weight? Eventually he'll just waste away.'

'I know it's trite but if there's anything I can do?'

'Thanks. You do enough for me already looking after Sprock.'

'That's no hardship, he's company for Henry.'

Two furry heads look up from under the table.

'They heard,' I say.

'More like they got a sniff of a cheese toastie.'

I hold out the crust to Sprocket and change the subject. 'I spoke to Nick earlier.'

'How is he?'

'You're a worse liar than him,' I say. 'I know you've been chatting.'

Linda shrugs and smiles. 'Yeah we have, spoke last night. He says he wants to meet Gareth. Says how about you come on a double date with us?'

'Really?' I say in surprise. 'He must really like you.'

She blushes, 'I really like him.'

'About time he settled down.'

She blushes even more. 'Well I don't know about that.'

'Well,' I say, 'according to my Dad, you're getting married.'

I rummage through the chest of drawers and select a few lightweight jumpers for Dad. I feel sad hunting through his belongings. He won't be coming back to the home that was his pride and joy. He loved this house, Mum did too. What are we going to do with the house, with all the stuff in it?

I pick up a photograph from the dressing table of him and Mum on their wedding day. They look impossibly young and fresh faced and so happy. I tuck the photograph in the holdall with the jumpers, he can have it on his bedside table. On impulse I pick up the one of Nick and I when I was three and Nick was a baby and add it to the bag. We'd obviously both just had haircuts before the picture was taken and my hair is so short I could be mistaken for a boy. I pick up the bag and turn the light out, it's only eight o'clock but the sky is dark and full of rain.

A newspaper folded over to the crossword is on the bedside cabinet. I pick it up and see the familiar blue pen that Dad always used. Only one clue has been answered but then scribbled out. Dad used to do the crossword every day and proudly claimed that he always completed it. He still has the paper every day, but he doesn't read it, says the letters won't keep still on the page. I put it back on the bedside table, unwillingly to throw it away.

As I come down the stairs a feeling comes over me that I'm not alone, that there is someone else in the house. I give myself a mental shake, Dad's frightened warnings about danger have obviously spooked me more than I thought. I should have brought Sprocket with me for company.

I put the holdall on the floor by the front door and

a noise from the lounge makes my stomach flip. I stand still and listen; I can definitely hear something. Is there someone in there? Shall I just open the front door and go? Don't be so stupid; of course there's no one in there. Anyway, I've left my handbag in there and my car keys are in it, so I have no choice. I take a deep breath and slowly push open the lounge door with my foot, I can't see anything but can still hear that noise. I walk in slowly and pick up my handbag from the sofa where I left it. What is that noise?

Relief floods me as I look over at the window, a bee is buzzing up and down between the net curtain and the glass frantically trying to get out. I walk over and open the window and shoo it out, smiling to myself. I always did let my imagination run away with me. What an idiot. I close the window and go back out into the hall and pick up the holdall.

I'm just about to open the front door when the doorbell rings. Damn, who is that? I stand very still, hoping that whoever it is will go away. The bell rings again and the letterbox is rattled. The shadowy silhouette of a head through the opaque glass in the door looms larger and I take a quick step backwards as a nose is pressed up against the window. I quietly lower the holdall to the floor.

They won't be able to see me, will they? I feel stupid now and wish I'd just opened the door. The nose is unpressed and I breathe a sigh of relief. The letterbox rattles again and I realise with horror that whoever is there is going to look through. I swiftly step forward and duck down and hold the internal letterbox flap shut and I feel the pressure of fingers pressing against it as they try to force it open. After what seems like forever the pressure is gone and I hear the clunk of the letterbox being dropped and the light in the hallway changes as whoever it is walks away.

I hold my crouched position until my legs start to ache and then walk backwards into the lounge and park myself on the sofa. What an idiot, why didn't I just open the door? Whoever it was is certainly nosy. I sit back and close my eyes, if I leave now whoever it was will see me and I'll feel even more stupid.

I'm pondering as to why I care what some random person might think of me when the doorbell rings again; whoever it is they're back. I could hide in here, but I feel embarrassed by my own behaviour, so I go out into the hall and open the door.

'Hello Louise.' It's the next-door neighbour.

'Oh, hello Simon. Did you ring earlier? Only I was upstairs sorting stuff out and thought I might have heard the bell but wasn't sure.' Doesn't even sound convincing to my own ears. I'm sure my face is glowing beetroot red too.

'No, wasn't me,' he says. 'Saw your car and just called round to see how you are and how Tom's getting on?'

'Oh, I'm fine, Dad's not too bad.'

'Eileen said they're still doing tests or something. Is he any better? Do you think he'll be coming back home soon?'

'Probably not for a while, it's still early days,' I lie. I don't want to tell him or discuss it. I don't want it to be true, or real.

'If there's anything Eileen and I can do you've only to ask. We can keep an eye on the house, cut the grass and suchlike.'

'Thank you, that's very kind of you but don't

worry about the grass, Brendan's offered to do it.'

'Oh, has he, okay. Not sure what Tom would say – you know he's not keen on him.' He seems put out, annoyed. This pleases me, but why? Because I don't like him, I suddenly realise. I don't like him or his wife very much – never had a lot to do with them but they're odd. I always found Simon a bit smarmy and insincere and Eileen, well, she's just odd. A cold and strange fish. I know Dad saw a lot of them, Simon in particular, but I've never had much to do with them.

'Brendan offered, it would have seemed rude to refuse.'

'Of course, no problem, just thought I'd offer. Not got your dog with you today?' Why doesn't he just go away?

'No, not today.' Sprocket never took to him; you can't fool a dog, they know when someone doesn't like them. For some reason I notice that Simon dyes his hair, it's a strange orangey brown. Apricot. That's it, apricot. Perhaps Eileen does it for him.

'Give Tom our regards, won't you? Let us know when he's up for a visit and we'll pop and see him, cheer the old fella up.' He brushes his hair back from his forehead in a nervous gesture. His hands have freckly, bumpy skin and are covered in fine hair. There's something repellent about them, they remind me of a baby orangutan.

'Yes, I will.' I smile. 'Thanks.' Go away.

At last he takes the hint and turns to walk down the drive and in that split second, I remember, bang, as if a light has gone on. The back of his head, that strange apricot hair, I know where I've seen it before.

He turns and raises his hand in a wave and I stare at him and try to keep the shock from showing on my face. I give a feeble wave and quickly close the front door. I lean my head against the cool glass, my heart pounding and a rushing in my ears.

The last time I saw Suzanne Jenkins she was going into the house next door to Linda. The house for sale. But what I've only just remembered was that there was someone walking in front of her, I could just see the top of his head. Someone with strange apricot coloured hair.

Is it him? Is he the Frogham throttler? He can't be can he? My Dad's perfectly ordinary-estate-agent-next-door neighbour? Maybe I'm being ridiculous, but I must tell Gareth. I fumble in my handbag for my phone, so much junk in there. There it is; I pull out one of Sprocket's nibbled rubber bones, I fling it back in and rummage again.

'Oh, dear,' says a voice from behind me. I freeze and turn around. Simon is standing in the kitchen doorway.

I stare at him open mouthed, how did he get in?

'How...?'

'You're wondering how I got in?' He cuts me off, grinning, he holds up a key and dangles it from his fingers as if it were a prize. 'Back door key. Tom gave me it. I persuaded him to in case he ever took ill.' He smiles a small, cold smile.

'What are you doing here?' My voice is quivering. I feel sick.

'Oh, I think you know, Louise. I think you know. I wasn't sure, thought maybe I'd got away with it. But your face gave you away as I left. You'd be no good at poker.'

Oh. My. God. It is him. I stare in shock, my feet rooted to the floor.

He steps closer and I stupidly step back towards the stairs. The front door, why didn't I open the front door and run? Too late, too late.

'So now,' he says, raising his eyebrows, 'the question is what are we going to do about it?'

I'm going to die.

Chapter Sixteen

'You should have kept your nose out. Left well alone.'

'I… I don't know what you mean. What do you think I've done?' I'm playing for time. I hope.

'Going to my house on Tuesday. Did you think I wouldn't know? I saw you, remember?' His mouth is twisted into an ugly sneer.

'I was taking the post round, that's all.' I edge backwards to the stairs.

'That's what *she* said. But I know when someone's spying on me. And your face just confirmed it.'

'No, no, I wasn't spying on you.'

'Anyway,' he goes on in a conversational tone, 'I was going to wait a while until the next one, but you've spoilt that now.'

I watch as he pulls a knife from his trouser pocket. It's not a big knife, probably six inches long, but it's long enough; the blade sharp and shiny. He has surprisingly well muscled arms. I've always thought of him as weedy.

'Thought I'd have a change this time, do a bit of cutting instead of throttling.' He chuckles to himself. 'The Frogham Throttler, who thought that up? You?'

'Don't say anymore. Let me go and I won't tell anyone.' Lame and desperate but anything is worth a try.

'We both know you will.'

'Did you use that key to come in here and frighten Dad?' I need to keep him talking.

'Yeah. It was fun. You should have seen his face when he came downstairs in the middle of the night and found all the lights and the TV on. He nearly caught me one time. Just managed to get out of the back door in time. Old fool.'

I feel a flash of anger, poor Dad. 'He's not an old fool, he's ill, and you were supposed to be his friend. You came in here and terrorised him.'

He snorts, 'Friend? Tight old bastard. I offered him a good price for that land. But would he take it? No, he wouldn't. Nobody needs a garden that big. His shed has been very useful though, but he knew someone had been in there. I managed to persuade him it was Herman Munster next door. Didn't take much persuading either. I knew he was getting forgetful so let's just say I helped confuse him a bit more. It couldn't have suited me better when he went into hospital.'

'You're sick. And what about the shed? There's nothing in the shed.' I'm stalling for time. I dread to think about what might have been in Dad's shed.

'Not now. Nothing to incriminate me now. Watched that retard Brendan fawning all over you and that dog the other day. Sickening. He owes me a padlock.'

That's why Sprocket was whining, he could tell he was there.

'But enough of that. Must get on. Eliminate the problem.'

'Why? Why did you kill those women?'

''Why?' He looks up at the ceiling, enjoying himself. 'Why not? It was too easy, those fools in the police are nowhere near catching me and to be honest after the first one I quite enjoyed it. Although she was an accident. Poor Suzie.'

I hear myself gasp when he says her name.

'Got ideas above her station, wasn't happy with being a bit on the side, reckoned she was going to tell my wife so we could start a new life together.' His face twists into a sinister sneer. 'Well I didn't want to start a new life, quite happy with the one I've got.' He looks at me. 'It won't work you know.'

'What won't work?'

'Trying to keep me talking, I know what you're trying to do but it's pointless, no-one is going to rescue you.'

'I've told the police.'

'What?' He looks uncertain for the first time. 'What have you told them?'

'You. I told them about you.'

He studies my face, looks me up and down. 'You're a useless liar. If you'd told them I'd have been arrested by now.'

'I told them I saw Suzanne going into that house for sale, in Conyers Road.'

He frowns. 'Hmm, even if you have it might be problematic, but not insurmountable. But, anyway…' He advances towards me. 'That's not going to save you, it'll take weeks to connect that to me. By which time you'll be very dead.'

He's right. By the time Linda raises the alarm it'll be too late. She'll just think I'm sorting stuff out for Dad and it's taking longer than I thought.

'But I like an audience, so I'll tell you, we've plenty of time,' he points at me with the knife, 'The funny thing is I nearly got caught by your idiot friend with the poodle.'

He laughs at my surprise.

'You've not got all of it worked out have you? I left Suzie's body in the house next door to your friend, the hippy one with the dog. We used to meet there and then, ah, things got out of hand, and she had to die. Which was fine until the house was sold and I had to move her. I'd just hauled her out into the backyard to put her in my car and that poodle ran in and starting sniffing around and barking at me.'

So, he beat Norman up.

'That idiot followed it in to see what it was barking at. I'm stood there with Suzie's body rolled up in an old blanket, so I had to do something. I went out and jumped him before he could come in and catch me. He's lucky I didn't kill him. I did think about it but then it would have been another body to get rid of.' He shrugs and raises his eyebrows. Bastard is enjoying this.

'But why did you take his dog?' More pathetic stalling from me, even though he's told me it's pointless.

'Fucking thing bit me.' His lip curls in a sneer. 'Chased after me and was trying to defend that idiot. Picked it up and put it in the boot, I was going to kill it but changed my mind. Didn't want the mess. I let it out of the boot after I'd dumped Suzie's body.'

'You're sick.'

'Anyway,' he says, stepping towards me, 'much as I love to chat I must get on.'

'Glenda.' I shout, stepping back. 'Why Glenda?'

'Why not? She wanted to buy a rental, showed her around a few properties but she treated me like her lackey. Kept giving me the come on and then got all offended when I made a pass at her. Snooty bitch. Said she was going report me. Couldn't have that. Wasn't so snooty by the time I'd finished with her.'

'Oh God.' I can feel myself shaking.

He stares at me and puts his head to one side. 'Enough talking.'

I'm still holding my handbag and I tighten my grip on it; the glimmer of a plan floating around in my head.

He holds up the knife and turns the blade this way and that, scrutinising it.

'Yes. I think I'm going to enjoy this. You might not.'

My insides turn to jelly and with trembling hands I swing my handbag at him and let it go. I race up the stairs and as I get to the landing I can hear his feet thundering up behind me. Run! My brain is screaming, run! I hesitate too long, and I feel him grab my hair from behind. I wrench myself free leaving him with a handful of hair, my scalp smarting. He stumbles backwards down the stairs and I look around the landing frantically wondering where to go. The bathroom has a lock, but he'll soon break that down. Mind made up I race into the back bedroom and slam the door. I look round desperately for something to put up against the door. I don't have long.

Nick's old single bed, a heavy oak chest of drawers and dressing table. With strength I didn't know I had I drag and pull the chest of drawers from under the window across the room. I silently pray that I can block the door before he gets to it. With pushing and shoving I force it across the doorway and wedge it under the handle. It won't stop him for long; I look around for something else: the bed.

I grab the end of the bedstead and pull, nothing. I heave again but it won't budge. I waste valuable seconds standing staring at the bed wondering what to do. I massage my scalp where he pulled out my hair, my hand comes away bloody.

I wish I had my mobile phone. Damn! I curse myself for throwing my handbag at him. But I had to do something, it was all I had.

It's very quiet, I thought he'd be breaking the door down by now.

I tiptoe to the door and put my ear against the wood.

Silence.

Is he trying to fool me to get me to come out? Where is he?

I dash over and look out of the window to see if he's outside; the garden is empty. I try the handles to open them. The windows are solid UPVC windows with double glazed shatter proof glass, I yank harder on the handles and they don't even move. Locked. Where are the keys? I pull open the drawers and move the clothes around, run my hand along the bookshelves. Nothing. I could search for hours and not find them.

Perhaps I could break the windows with something? I look for something heavy, there's an old wooden footstool; I pick it up and swing it by the wooden legs at the window. It bounces off. I swing it again and again, but it makes no impression at all.

Oh God.

I run over to the door and put my ear to it again.

Silence.

What's he doing out there? Has he gone? Even if I

could break a window he could be waiting outside. But I could scream if I could get it open, maybe someone would hear me.

Why would he go? I'm trapped in here, he can take his time.

I look out of the window and curse the fact that the house isn't overlooked at all. I could stand at the window naked and be sure that no-one would see me. Even if Brendan were in his garden he wouldn't be able to see me as the trees are so overgrown.

I hear a noise from the door. It sounds like hammering.

Think.

THINK.

I can't think. I'm going to die. I don't want to die.

He's there now.

At the door.

The banging's getting louder.

A weapon, I need a weapon.

I pull open drawers and rummage through them, nothing. The wardrobe is full of clothes. Only clothes, of course.

Maybe a coat hanger could be a weapon, if I can find a wire one. I frantically pull jackets, coats and shirts from the hangers flinging them to the floor. Wooden hangers, padded silk hangers but no wire hangers. Useless.

I spy Mum's sewing basket on the dressing table, there must be scissors in there. I rush across the room and try to open it, but my fingers won't work and I can't undo the clasp on the box.

Oh God. The hammering's getting louder and I hear the splinter of wood. I look at the door and see the blunt end of a lump hammer poking through the wood. That explains the silence, he must have gone and got the hammer. The wood cracks and splinters as the hammer is pulled out and swung again.

I finally manage to wrench open the sewing box and empty the contents onto the floor. I fall to my knees and run my hands over the contents.

Scissors!

I pick them up and slip my fingers into the handles and almost sob with frustration – they're pinking shears, blunt ended, completely useless.

Needles. Useless.

But hang on what's that.

A gun.

Dad's Luger. In Mum's sewing box.

I pick it up with both hands, it's heavy.

Bullets, where are the bullets?

I don't know but it doesn't matter, I wouldn't know how to load it anyway. Perhaps I can hit him with it. Or break the window.

Another loud splinter. There's a small hole in the door and he's looking through it at me. I look away, I can't be distracted, I don't have time.

I turn the gun round and hold it by the barrel, I get up and stand in front of the window and bash the gun against glass with all my strength. The faintest hairline crack appears.

Yes!

I can do this.

More noise from the door, I look over to see Simon's head emerging through the hole. He looks at me and laughs showing greying teeth. His face is flushed and sweat is running down his face.

I turn and hit the window again and again with the gun as hard as I can, my shoulders aching with the effort, more hairline cracks appear. I can hear someone whimpering.

It's me.

Simon's barking laughter grows louder.

I keep hitting the window and more cracks appear but they're tiny and when I push my hands against them they don't even move. The futility of it all hits me.

It's useless, I can't get out.

I'm going to die.

I turn the gun around and hold it by the handle and point it at him.

'Not that old thing. Give up Louise, make it easier on yourself.'

The hole in the door is bigger now, he pulls his head back through and I hear more wood being yanked away from it then the swing of the hammer again. Satisfied that the hole is big enough he clambers through onto the chest of drawers. He sits there for a moment catching his breath, watching me.

He jumps down and comes towards me and I back away as far away as I can, until the window sill cuts into my back and I can go no further. I'm trapped.

'Well, you've made it more difficult than it should have been Louise, and I'm afraid you'll have to pay for that.' He's getting closer and I can smell the sweat on him, the heat radiating from his body. He runs a sweaty hand through his apricot hair.

I point the gun at him with both hands.

'Don't come any closer or I'll shoot.'

He throws back his head and laughs.

'Go ahead, it's not even loaded.'

I put my finger on the trigger. 'I will, I'll shoot you.'

He pulls the knife from his pocket and runs his finger along the blade. 'Let the fun begin.'

A strange feeling of calm settles over me.

This is it, this is how it ends.

Goodbye world.

I close my eyes and pull the trigger.

Chapter Seventeen

I can't see.

There's a deafening, ringing noise.

Blackness.

Am I dead?

The ringing turns to banging.

I open my eyes. Bright white light. Am I in heaven?

The white light gradually turns into the white artex on the ceiling.

I'm not dead. I'm lying on the floor by the window, still holding the gun in my hand.

Someone's screaming. Is it me?

I swallow. No, it's not me.

My head hurts, I slowly turn and see Simon lying on the floor by the door, he's screaming and rolling around, there's blood, lots of blood. The blood is seeping into the green and pink roses on the carpet, turning them black. A part of me wonders why I'm noticing this.

He sees me looking at him. 'You fucking bitch, you shot me! Get me some help. I'm dying.'

I sit up and the room spins momentarily.

I slowly stand up and step towards him.

The gun *was* loaded.

'Help me!' he screams. 'Help me, you sick bitch.'

'You'll live,' a cold voice says. 'A bullet in the leg

won't kill you.' I realise the cold voice is mine.

The banging is getting louder, it's coming from downstairs. It's the sound of a battering ram breaking down the front door.

'Help me,' snivels Simon.

'I don't think so.' I stand over him and point the gun at his chest.

'No, no, please don't kill me.' He screams and yelps. Like a dog.

'You were going to kill me,' I say.

He pulls himself upright on his elbows and scrabbles backwards dragging his injured leg. Blood pumps over the floor.

The sound of splintering wood as the front door caves in and then voices shouting my name.

Simon looks at me and smiles. 'Too late, bitch,' he hisses.

I take aim and pull the trigger and enjoy the look of horror on his face.

Click.

No bullets.

The thump of feet running up the stairs, men shouting.

'Louise! My God! Louise.' Gareth climbs through the hole yelling orders at people I can't see. 'In here! She's in here!'

I watch him come towards me, but I am unable to move. He looks down at Simon and moves me away from him then gently prises my fingers from the gun and gathers me in his arms.

'Thank God you're alive.' His face is grey. I can feel him shaking.

I let him hold me, my arms dangling uselessly by my sides. I can't speak, I'm exhausted, utterly spent.

Numb. My fingers ache. I rest my head into his chest.

A uniformed policeman climbs through the hole then swiftly moves the chest of drawers away from the door to let several others in. Suddenly the room is crowded. Two of them kneel next to Simon, while the third radios for an ambulance.

'You don't need to handcuff me. I'm injured.' Simon is squealing at the officer.

The officer ignores him, and I watch as he pulls the cuffs tighter, Simon squeals again. The officer's mouth is set in a grim, tight line.

'Come on, let's get you out of here.' I walk on jellied legs as Gareth half carries me down the stairs and into the lounge. He lowers me gently onto the sofa and I sit and stare into space.

'You're in shock, Louise. We'll get the doctor to have a look at you when he gets here.' He picks up Dad's tartan rug from his chair and puts it over me.

And all I can think is; I wanted to kill him, as I pulled the trigger I wanted him to die for what he'd done. I wasn't thinking about what would happen to me, I just wanted him dead. If the gun had been loaded with another bullet I would have killed him.

That feeling cannot be undone.

I'm as bad as him.

'I don't understand how you knew it was him,' I say. 'How did you know?'

It's Saturday afternoon and I'm at home, Gareth arrived an hour ago, Sprocket is lying across my feet snoozing and I'm snuggled up safe and warm in Gareth's arms.

He massages his forehead with his fingers and I think how tired he looks.

But it's over now.

Gareth can't be personally involved with me and continue to run the murder investigation so has handed it over to another officer. I think he's a bit disappointed that he doesn't get to finish the job, but the bonus is that after two long days of handing over and debriefing he's on leave.

When I gave my statement at the station, we went over and over what happened so many times that I thought I was going to scream. Every tiny detail; details that I wasn't even aware that I knew.

And it was all true, except for one small detail.

I told them that the first shot I fired was empty and that the second shot was the one that hit Simon in the leg.

Yesterday was a blur. I vaguely remember Nick arriving home, there seemed to be lots of cups of tea made that I didn't drink and meals that I didn't eat. I was in shock but today I feel better, not so numb.

Today is the first time I've seen Gareth since it all happened. We sat together on Dad's sofa until the ambulance arrived and once the paramedic had checked me over I was given a hot, sweet cup of tea by a WPC and taken in the back of a police car to the station. As we turned the corner onto the main road I recognised Rupert's car coming towards me, so someone had obviously tipped him off. I quickly looked down, so my hair covered my face. I didn't want to be a headline in the paper I work for.

'Your sighting of Suzanne Jenkins going into the house next door to Linda clinched it. We were closing in on him, but we wouldn't have got there so quickly without your tip off. We knew Glenda had some house viewings lined up and we were trawling through the estate agents.' He pulls me closer. 'To think I nearly lost you. It doesn't bear thinking about.'

'But how did you know where I was? Where he was?' My brain is fuddled, I can't make sense of it.

'He wasn't at work, so we went to his house,' he explains. 'I started to worry then, I knew you were going to your Dad's. When his wife opened the door - the look on her face, she knew. When we asked where he was she just caved and told us he'd gone next door. I think she was relieved. Actually, I think she quite enjoyed it once she realised he'd never be coming home again.'

He pulls me closer, Sprocket snores louder.

'I feared the worst then; I've never felt so afraid in all my life. I was making all sorts of deals with God as we broke down the door.' We hold each other tight, not speaking.

I look up at Gareth, this work-weary inspector, who must have seen so much in his career, and he feared losing me. I hug him tighter.

'Dad knew something was wrong, but he got the wrong person,' I say.

'He did, Simon manipulated your Dad to make him think it was the other neighbour. Forensics are taking the shed apart – looks like he used it to store the bodies for a while.'

The bastard, Dad thought he was his friend. I almost wish there had been another bullet in the gun.

'His wife knew? She knew all along?'

'Suspected, although she's playing dumb now. Probably too frightened of him to do anything.'

'The fake Scottish lady,' I say suddenly. 'The phone calls to the newspaper, they were her!'

'She's not admitting anything, but yes, more than

likely.'

How could she? Because of her Glenda died and I would too if it wasn't for Dad's Luger.

'Anyway, once he's out of hospital he'll tell us everything. He knows he's going to prison for the rest of his life so there's no use denying it. As for his wife, time will tell whether the CPS decide to prosecute her.'

I snuggle into Gareth's neck and close my eyes.

'Louise?' Gareth says hesitantly.

'Mmm?'

'Did you know the gun was loaded?'

I pull away and look up at him.

'No. Nick took the bullets out of it weeks ago and hid them. Dad must have found them and loaded it, luckily for me.'

'It was.'

A sudden thought hits me. 'Will I be charged? For shooting him?'

'No. Self-defence, no need to worry.'

'That's a relief.' I snuggle back into Gareth's neck.

By the time the other policemen came in Gareth had moved me away from Simon. Simon was screaming that I tried to kill him but everyone surmised it was self-defence.

'It's a very old gun. Difficult to be sure which chamber was fired first. But they've no reason to look,' Gareth reassures me.

'You sure you're up for visiting?'

'Of course, I am. Stop fussing Nick, I'm absolutely fine and I want to see Dad.'

We're outside Blossom Unit waiting to be buzzed in.

'Just don't want you overdoing it. I should have been here.'

'For God's sake, stop feeling so guilty. I'm fine and you need to stop beating yourself up about it.' He's been like this ever since he got back yesterday.

I go through and hold the door open for him. 'I wonder if Dad has seen it on the news? Do you think we should tell him if he hasn't?'

'Don't know,' says Nick, 'see how he is? Depends whether he's away with the fairies or not.'

We can't see Dad as we go in, so we carry on round to his room.

'Hello Dad.' He's sitting in his chair looking out of the window at the tree.

'Oh, hello you two,' he gets up. 'It's been all go here, today.'

'Been busy then Dad?' Nick settles himself in the other chair. I suppose I'm sitting on the bed then.

'Been defusing a bomb.' He sits back down and crosses his arms.

'Really,' says Nick. 'How exciting.'

Dad then tells us in great detail how he and two others defused a bomb that they found under a table in the dining room. I find my mind drifting, his words becoming distant. An unaccountable feeling of sadness washes over me; sadness for Dad losing his mind in his twilight years, the pointless deaths of two women. The futility of it all.

'LOUISE!' Nick hisses at me, shaking me out of myself-pity.

'What?'

'Dad was just saying that he had a visitor.'

'I did.' Dad looks pleased with himself.

'What, today?'

Dad nods. 'Just before you got here. Been like Clapham Junction, it has.'

'Who?' I'm surprised they've let someone else in, they told us family only for the moment.

'You'll never guess.' He looks really pleased with himself.

'Jean?'

'No, not Jean. Simon.'

Nick raises his eyebrows at me.

'Oh, really? How was he?'

'Not happy. Not happy at all.' Dad seems to find this really funny.

'Why was that?' How are we even having this conversation?

'He's not happy with you, Louise.' He's really laughing now. I look at Nick whose eyebrows have nearly disappeared into his hair.

'He says you tried to kill him. I don't know, I think he's gone barmy.' he points his finger at his forehead. 'Not right in the head.'

I'm speechless, so say nothing. Dad must have seen the news of Simon's arrest on the TV. But he wouldn't have known he was shot; that was kept out of the public domain. And my name has been kept out of it totally, much to Ralph's disgust. Although I know it will all come out at the trial.

Dad's muttering under his breath.

'What's that Dad?' prompts Nick.

'I said,' Dad shouts, 'I never did like him much. Shifty.'

Nick and I look at each other and laugh. There's a hysterical quality to my laughter and I can't stop.

'What's so funny?' Dad's annoyed.

'Nothing, Dad.' I say. 'Nothing.' But I can't stop.

Tears run down my face and I get hiccups. It's only when I see Nick's concerned face that I manage to control myself.

'Anyway,' Dad is looking at me intently, 'the main thing is that you're okay. Simon's leg will mend and if it doesn't that's too bad, he got what he deserved.' How does he know? He couldn't possibly know.

'Lucky your policewoman friend was there.' He frowns at Nick. 'Although she left it to the last minute.' He sniffs.

It's all in there, jumbled up, but somehow, he knows.

'Anyway,' he goes on, 'you know what you have to do now. Or not do. The choice is yours.'

Nick looks at me, 'What? What's he on about?'

I shrug my shoulders, 'I don't know.'

But I do.

'How the hell could he know? About Simon being shot? Any of it? How?' I ask as we walk across the car park to the car, Nick shaking his head in disbelief.

'I don't know, but he does.'

'And what was that about your choice?'

'No idea.'

'Chipper though, wasn't he? Seemed happy even though he's away with the fairies. A nice visit.'

It was a nice visit. After telling us Simon has visited Dad then went on to tell us about the tigers in the garden again and we all laughed together and yes, it was all nonsense, but Dad was happy. He doesn't really know where he is or why he's there, but he's content. He's in cloud cuckoo land and nothing can touch him or hurt him now.

'Nick.'

'Hmm?'

'I've got something to tell you.'

We both stop, and he looks at me.

'Shit. You're not ill, are you?'

'No, I'm not. Look, let's get in the car and I'll tell you.'

When we reach the car, we get in and sit in silence.

'Come on then, don't keep me in suspense.'

'Okay.' I take a deep breath.

So I tell him, all of it. And as I tell him he doesn't speak, and when I've finished he buries his head in his hands.

Should I have told him? I don't know. I only know that I can't carry this secret around with me for the rest of my life. Mum is dead, before too long Dad won't even know who we are, so that just leaves Nick and I, and my real mother.

'I'm sorry, so, so sorry.' I put my hand on Nick's arm. 'I wish I could have spared you this, but I can't keep it a secret any longer, Nick.'

He doesn't speak, and I think: I've lost him; I've lost my brother who means everything to me.

Nick wipes his eyes with his hands, his face is wet with tears and I wish I could take back my words.

'You're sure? You're sure this is all true?'

'Yes. Everything fits. Dates, circumstances. Dad's confession.'

'You can't trust that,' he almost laughs.

'No. But I believe it's all true.'

'I don't even know why I asked, of course it's true.' He looks rueful.

'It's a hell of a shock. I've had a few weeks to get used to it.'

'Fuck me. Shock's a bit of an understatement.'

241

We look at each other and then we start to laugh; at the absurdity of it all, the insane unbelievability of it.

But mostly we laugh, because we're family; because he's my brother and I'm his sister and whatever happens, we'll face it together.

Epilogue

I lived here long ago, although I have no memory of it.

The houses in Ravenscroft Avenue are three floors high with large bay windows and coloured tiles in the front porches. Low brick walls surround the front gardens and ageing, knobbly trees lift the paving slabs under my feet.

I've walked past number twenty-four three times now trying to find the courage to knock on the door. I'm feeling slightly paranoid and wonder if curtains are twitching, so, on the fourth pass I take a deep breath and veer off the pavement without stopping, open the gate, march up the path and climb the three steps to the front door.

The door is big, much wider and taller than my own and painted a glossy black with a shiny chrome letterbox and knocker. Either side of the porch old, stone plant pots can barely contain the huge leafy plants that tumble out of them. This house is not one of the shabby ones, it is loved and well looked after and I feel a surprising stab of envy. Envy for the life I could have lived, the family I could have had.

Right, here goes. I grab the knocker with my clammy fingers and because I'm so nervous I bang it much too hard. The sound reverberates behind the door.

I try to steady my breathing to slow my pounding heart. I take a deep breath and exhale slowly through my nose, hearing the air as it escapes my nostrils.

I wait. And wait. I'm already turning to leave when the door is opened.

And there she is.

'Yes?' she says, making it a question.

She's taller than I expected and looks younger too, and a part of me remembers. She's waiting for me to speak but all I can do is stare. She looks annoyed and I expect the door to shut at any moment.

'Can I help you?' She sounds uncertain now, her eyes search my face and she nervously flutters her hand to cover her mouth. Does she recognise me? Is there a faint trace of something about me that is familiar to her?

My throat is so dry that it hurts to swallow, as if my body is trying to stop me from speaking.

What I say next will change lives forever.

Time seems to slow down; there's a stillness in the air. It feels as though we're in a bubble; the only two people in the world. I stare at her and she stares back with eyes that look so familiar; eyes that are just like mine. Does she see it? Does she know what I'm about to say? Is that hope that I see in her eyes?

When I start to speak my voice is hoarse and as I say the words she takes her hand from her mouth and begins to cry.

'Hello,' I say, 'I think I'm your daughter.'

THE END

Thank you so much for reading this book. I really do appreciate it. I am an Indie Author, not backed by a big publishing company. This is my debut novel and if you've enjoyed reading it I'm genuinely thrilled. I've worked hard to eliminate any typos and errors, but if you spot any, please let me know:
marinajohnson2017@outlook.com.

If you enjoyed this book please leave a review on Amazon and if you think your friends would enjoy reading it, please share it with them.

Many thanks

Marina Johnson

Lewy Bodies Dementia

Lewy Bodies Dementia impairs thinking, memory, executive function (planning, processing information), or the ability to understand visual information. Patients with LBD may have fluctuations in attention or alertness; problems with movement including tremors, stiffness, slowness and difficulty walking; hallucinations; and alterations in sleep and behaviour.
Progressively debilitating, LBD can also cause people to experience visual hallucinations or act out their dreams.
https://www.lbda.org/

Printed in Great Britain
by Amazon